Dr. Aristotle Campbell i
brother has been abducte
find him. Forced out of 1
laboratory, Ari must leave

and search the farthest reaches of space for his other half. He hastily equips himself with a flawlessly tied cravat, a handful of clues, and his small science vessel. Now, all he needs is a pilot to get him across the Verge, a barrier separating the civilized world from ungoverned space.

Pilot Orin Stone is a desperate man. No ship, no pay, no prospects. He spends his days barely scraping by in the rough colonies lining the Verge interior. When he gets an offer from a frantic, upper-crust professor in need of a pilot, he has no choice but to take the job. He just can't believe it when the professor turns out to be the most gorgeous man he's ever seen and that his offer includes a ship of Orin's own. If Orin can keep his heart (and other portions of his anatomy) from leaping every time sweet, innocent Dr. Campbell looks at him, this should be his easiest job yet.

Rugged Orin and aristocratic Ari work together to navigate the lawless areas of space beyond the Verge, soon discovering that they work well together in all areas. Their immediate and intense attraction to one another is an obstacle to their plans that neither saw coming. More than sparks will fly when they break through the force field and enter restricted space, all alone together for the perilous journey, leaving barriers to their growing attachment far behind.

In their search across the stars, can two desperate men find their home in one another?

RESTRICTED

The Verge, Book One

A.C. Thomas

A NineStar Press Publication

www.ninestarpress.com

Restricted

Printed in the USA

Print ISBN: 978-1-64890-129-4

First Edition, November, 2020

Also available in eBook, ISBN: 978-1-64890-128-7

WARNING:
This book contains sexually explicit content, which may only be suitable for mature readers.

For my family, who believe in me.
(Please ignore all sex scenes and replace with chess.)

Chapter One

"You want me to do what?"

Ari straightened his shoulders, hands folded together on the table between them, suppressing a wince as his skin stuck unpleasantly to a thick smear of residue best left uninvestigated.

Somewhere behind him the sound of glass breaking was followed by a bowel-shaking roar, a meaty impact, scuffling sounds, and hearty guffaws.

Definitively best left uninvestigated.

He sniffed quietly, regretting the action as the odor of stale beer and unwashed bodies assaulted his senses. Forcing himself to meet his companion's bored regard, he cleared his throat before speaking in as firm a tone as he could manage.

"In the interest of saving both of our time, I'll cut to the chase. I require a pilot capable of navigating uncharted areas with immediate availability and a willingness to negotiate a flexible pay schedule."

Mr. "Call me Orin, honey" Stone slumped back in his seat with careless, sprawling grace, the edge of one enormous scuffed leather boot sliding across the floor to rest a millimeter away from the polished black toes of Ari's spats.

"So, just so we're clear— You're asking me to find you a pilot ready to jump right across the Verge into the deepest, slimiest dark, for—and this is the bit that really sticks in my throat, pumpkin— You want me to find you some sap willing to do all that for, apparently, no pay."

Keen bourbon eyes swept Ari from head to toe, that restless boot finally edging just close enough to touch.

"You're cute, sugar. But you're off your rocker."

Ari's chair scraped against the floor as he jolted forward in his seat, one hand closing around the fraying cuff of Orin's greatcoat.

"This is a matter of utmost urgency. My brother is—" He paused to clear his throat after an embarrassing crack in his voice. "My brother is missing; he has been abducted by an Outlier fiend, and I am utilizing every resource at my disposal to ensure his safe return. My inquiries led me to you, with the assurance you could facilitate a jump with immediate effect. Now I demand that you either provide said assistance, or you cease wasting my time."

Orin fixated on the white-knuckled grip holding his sleeve. The coiled strength of his thick forearm underscored Ari's awareness that he could break free at a moment's notice with very little energy expended.

"What kind of resources are we talking, here?" Orin's eyes narrowed under a heavy brow, the sweep of space-black lashes unexpectedly elegant against his brutish visage.

Ari drew a long breath, attempting to steady his resolve.

"I possess a three-year-old Xalanthe Explorer model 953V. It is in exemplary condition, and I am prepared to offer it as payment upon my brother's safe return to our home on Britannia."

Before he finished speaking, Orin sat up in his chair, the full extent of his imposing size suddenly evident even while seated. He turned his hand in Ari's grip, long fingers wrapping easily around his thin wrist.

"You're trading your ship. A brand-new ship. To any asshole willing to fly it? Just to finish a little game of hide-and-seek with your brother who—no offense, Red—sounds like he ran off with a bit of strange?"

Aristotle bristled, slim shoulders rising to his ears as the heat of an angry flush spread from the unfortunate ginger of his precisely parted hairline down to the white of his starched collar points.

"He did not 'run off'! He was abducted. I have no more time to waste with your nonsense, sir. Are you able to assist in my endeavor, or shall I continue pursuing a pilot on my own?"

A lopsided grin spread across his companion's face, revealing a hint of prominent canine and a surprisingly charming set of dimples. Orin gave another insolent sweep of his gaze, sticking to the length of Ari's throat rising above his cravat. The rumble of his voice dropped low enough that Ari had to strain to hear him above the surrounding chaos.

"Hmm, that depends, Red. That blush go all the way down?"

The clatter of the cheap aluminum chair against the cracking concrete floor was lost in the cacophony of raucous laughter, clinking glasses, and blaring synth music that characterized drinking establishments on the rough ring of colonies lining the Verge. Ari wrenched his arm away as he stood, breaking free.

He turned his back, adjusting his waistcoat with trembling fingers as he wracked his brain for alternative solutions. He had only taken a half step away from the table when a firm grip on his coattails wrenched him backward. He swung around, fists in a pugilist's stance, raised to the smiling face of Mr. Stone.

"Whoa now, slow up there, professor. If you're wanting to trade a whole damn ship for the temporary services of some sleazy sack of shit with a pilot's license, I got just the guy you need."

Knees weak with relief, Ari nearly attempted to sit before remembering he had overturned his chair, which was now likely glued to the filthy floor of the saloon.

"Excellent. Where can I find this person?"

That lopsided grin opened up into a full-blown smile, revealing rows of white, uneven teeth. "You're looking at him, sweetheart."

Ari twitched at the endearment, unaccustomed to the way they seemed to drip from the pilot's every phrase like butter melting off the plate.

He turned fully to face him, coattails twining around his narrow hips as Orin maintained his grip, tugging once with a waggle of thick brows at Ari's resulting unintentional pelvic thrust before releasing him with a flourish.

Orin pushed off from the table, broad shoulders rising up and up to just above Ari's line of sight. Ari swallowed an obvious comment on the pilot's intimidating height, realizing how much he'd underestimated the man's size.

Ari stared straight ahead at the hollow of Mr. Stone's throat, bronze skin left exposed by the open vee of his collarless shirt. A few dark, curling hairs peeked out of the opening, inches from Aristotle's nose. A strange fluttering sensation swept through his abdomen at the sight.

Recognizing the sensation as inappropriate at best and disastrous at worst, Ari turned on stiff legs and led the way out of the saloon, doing his utmost to avoid brushing up against the rough clientele. Heads swiveled to follow

Ari even as they ignored the much larger figure of Mr. Stone following close behind his every step.

Ari ducked his head as they emerged into the daylight, squinting against the intrusive brightness before heading off toward the nearest dry dock, zeroing in on his ship after a few minutes' walk. Mr. Stone was a silent shadow at his back, footsteps shockingly light for a man of his size.

The small exploratory vessel stood out among the busted-up freighters and speeders cluttering the dock. Clean panels of riveted steel shaped the subtle curves framing the centerpiece—a large frontal view screen. The only unnecessary ornament was that of the exaggerated dorsal fin, the sight of which had caused Aristotle's brother to laugh out loud when they first purchased the ship.

Ari's back stiffened at a low whistle, two familiar notes usually directed with prurient interest.

Mr. Orin Stone was circling his ship, one hand, large and square as a shovel head, trailing long fingers over the surface with surprising reverence.

"What's your name, beautiful?"

He directed his inquiry to the ship but turned to Aristotle as though expecting an answer.

Ari cleared his throat. "As I have previously mentioned, it is a Xalanthe—"

Orin cut him off with a rude sound pushed between full lips. "She."

Ari opened his mouth to reply, mistaking a brief pause for the conclusion of the pilot's statements.

"Ship's a she. And she's a pretty little thing, deserves a name. If you don't have one for her yet, I can think of something fancy to call her. Something with a bit of glitter to it. Little lady like this one deserves to shine."

His eyes in turn glittered at Ari, sparkling with amusement and apparent satisfaction upon viewing the small science vessel.

Without looking away, he spat into one rough palm before holding it out to Aristotle as if to shake.

"You've got yourself a deal, Red."

Ari recoiled from the offered hand, curling his own into protective fists at the notion of sealing a verbal contract with an exchange of bodily fluids.

"That is the most disgusting thing I have ever seen."

Orin's throaty laughter rang out against the polished metal panels of the ship exterior, echoing across the shipyard.

"Is it now? Well, stick with me, sugar; I could really expand your horizons."

Chapter Two

The ship's tour was short by necessity. The interior was built for efficiency, every space dedicated to a specific purpose.

Bay doors and the loading ramp led into the circular central room, dominated by the small galley with its modest multipurpose table and bench seating bolted to the floor off to the side. Storage chests lined the opposite wall.

On one side of the central room, a coded doorway led into the cockpit, pilot and copilot's seats arm's length apart with enough room surrounding each for a grown man to stand comfortably.

Ari eyed Orin surreptitiously, amending that to a grown man of average height and build, such as himself. Alright, so admittedly his build was definitely on the slender side of average, but he felt confident in his unremarkable height.

There was nothing about Mr. Stone's build that was unremarkable.

Ari tore his gaze away from Orin's broad hands as they caressed the controls on the deactivated dash, clearing his throat to continue the tour back through the galley and into the rear corridor.

The corridor was wider than one might have expected for a modest-sized vessel, but it was necessary for Ari to transport his storage crates of samples to and from the laboratory. The width was also sufficient for two men to stand shoulder to shoulder across. Ari mentally traced the sweeping lines of Orin's shoulders. It was also apparently just wide enough for one Mr. Stone and one Dr. Aristotle Campbell to stand with Mr. Stone's shoulders across and Aristotle's back flat against the wall.

Ari swallowed convulsively at the thought of Orin having him flat against the wall.

On one side of the corridor was Ari's room, a standard ship's bunk with en suite head complete with a sonic shower he could barely squeeze himself into.

On the other side was his brother's room. Theo had claimed the larger captain's quarters as both his bunk and workspace. Half again as large as Ari's room, his shelves of books and cluttered desk had dominated the space.

Prior to his disappearance, Theo's bed had practically become part of his desk, a Theo-shaped blank space the only concession to sleep amidst teetering piles of books and parchment.

In preparation for his search, Ari had cleared all but the bookshelves, carefully packing Theo's work into the storage crates now tucked beneath the floor panels of both their rooms.

Theo's en suite was also twice the size of Ari's, his sonic large enough for Ari to stand in without hitting the walls until he extended his arms past the elbow. He hoped Mr. Stone would be able to fit.

He also hoped he'd be able to stop picturing how Mr. Stone might fit into a shower stall. Stealing a glance at the pilot as he pushed thick waves of brown hair back off his face with a roguish grin, Ari knew it to be a false hope.

At the end of the corridor, another coded doorway led to the laboratory, a clean workspace of floor to ceiling storage panels and long workbench cluttered with equipment and samples.

All experiments had ceased upon Theo's disappearance, and in his haste, Ari had even mixed samples and destroyed months of work while searching for clues.

He cringed at the disorganization of the lab, but Mr. Stone simply looked it over with an impressed nod before heading back into the cockpit.

The pilot seemed entranced by the state-of-the-art flight controls, carefully pulling panels away here and there to study the inner workings.

Ari called attention to himself by snapping a roll of simulated parchment open across the dash.

Orin followed Ari's movements as he unfurled the collection of star maps. His gaze flicked up to Ari's face as he held out another roll of parchment. One broad thumb rubbed across the sharp edge of his jaw as Orin regarded the papers without making a move to accept them.

"What's all that?"

Ari shook the papers insistently, pushing them further into the pilot's space until large fingers wrapped around the roll.

"This is the ship's charter. Navigation is not my forte, so I will need you to check it over and make sure my calculations are sound. The remainder are charts I have fabricated in case we encounter Enforcers along the way, intended to indicate we have fallen off course rather than intentionally jumping the Verge. I attempted to procure emergency licensing, but I was denied. I can delay no longer, hence my need for your services."

Orin's eyebrows climbed as he studied the charter.

"Looks like more than a little jump across. Looks like you wanna go pretty far past the Verge. Ain't exactly easy to get through that big old force field, honey. Won't be an issue for me, but we're gonna have to come up with a plan to get you through the barrier. Everything about you screams Core, from the top of your combed-down hair to the tips of your shiny little shoes. Enforcers would never mistake you for a Verge rat like me. You look like you've never been out of the interior ring in your life."

Orin straightened up, turning to Ari with a serious expression, somehow all the more handsome for the shift in mood.

"Gonna have to fabricate more than a couple of maps for this. Besides, there's not much point to using maps if we're heading into the uncharted space of the deep dark. Gonna have to rely on my calculations to find our way out of there. You sure you wanna go through with all this? I gotta say, the deep dark just ain't a place for someone like you, professor. Seems to me you could barely handle our civilized life here in the colonies."

Ari crossed his arms over his chest, chin jutting defiantly. "An astounding assertion, having barely made my acquaintance. Just who do you suppose is 'someone like me,' Mr. Stone?"

Orin's eyes twinkled, mouth kicking up at one corner just enough to reveal a flash of dimple.

Ari was in no way charmed by it.

Orin took measured steps in a slow circle around Ari, heavy boots clunking against the metal floor in the restricted space of the cockpit.

"Someone like you is someone who grew up with a full belly and a solid roof. Nah, more than that. Bet you had servants, didn't you, sweetheart?"

Ari shrugged one shoulder, skin prickling as Orin circled behind him, sharply aware of his gaze tracing every line of his body. "We had a modest household staff when I was a child. My brother and I take bachelor's lodgings while planetside now, with only a housekeeper in our employ. All quite standard for our homeworld, I assure you."

Orin's snort was accompanied by the hushed sounds of him removing his heavy greatcoat and tossing it over the pilot's seat rather than hanging it on the dedicated coat peg as Ari had done upon entering the ship.

"Right. Someone like you is real used to being taken care of, used to having things when you want them, when you need them. There's none of that past the Verge, professor. Nothing so soft and pretty as yourself out there. Out there, fellas even rougher than me would give a lot for a go at a soft pretty thing like you."

Ari wrinkled his nose. "What precisely is that supposed to mean? A go?"

Ari's attention fell to the wide belt loops of Orin's broadcloth trousers as the pilot hooked his thumbs in them while leaning back to bray with laughter.

"Damn. You are precious, you know that, Red?"

Ari did his utmost to glare menacingly, to little effect. If he was honest with himself, all of these words and endearments were beginning to wear on him. No one had ever said anything remotely like that to Ari before, whether intended mockingly or complimentary. Obviously, none of it was sincere, it was immediately apparent that all of this was some strange affectation or quirk of speech. Perhaps it was common, out here in the harsher colonies. Certainly no one would speak that way back home on Britannia, or any other Core world for that matter.

Still. Hearing such language constantly directed at him was bafflingly impactful. He resolved to give his heart and other interested organs a stern talking-to at the earliest opportunity.

Mr. Stone studied him under his overgrown fringe, shaking his head to get his hair out of his eyes, the heavy waves immediately falling back into place despite his efforts.

Ari dropped his focus on Orin's hair to find Orin's regard as steady on his face as a hawk. When he spoke again, his voice was softer, careful and emphatic in a way that held every shred of Aristotle's attention.

"You sure about this? I wouldn't blame you if you back out right now, wouldn't even consider it going back on a deal. Seems like the decent thing to do here is to give you an opportunity to see nothing but my ugly backside as I get the hell off your ship, and you get yourself back to the safety of your little Core world."

Ari shook his head, chin jutting out in the way that drove Theo up the wall during an argument. "I'm afraid that won't be possible, Mr. Stone. My brother has need of me, and I will not fail him. I am also not the sort of gentleman who is willing to go back upon his word. I struck a deal with you, and I shall uphold it."

The smile that spread across Orin's face at that lit a fire behind his eyes, glowing softly in Ari's direction.

He nodded decisively, chucking Ari lightly beneath the chin. "You can put that stubborn little thing away, sweetheart. Deal's a deal. If you're so surefire set on this, then I'm not stopping you. First things first, let's get this pretty lady in shape. Anything needs doing before we head out for supplies?"

Ari rubbed his hand over his jaw, soothing the strange tingle of awareness that spread across his face from Orin's touch.

"I've been having a spot of trouble with getting it up to speed. We'll need to get a ship's mechanic to look at the engines as soon as possible."

Orin shook his head before Ari finished speaking. "Nah, no call for that. I can fix her up better than any crooked Verge mechanic you're gonna find around here. Where's her access panel?"

Ari led the way into the corridor, hesitating for a moment before bending to release the catch on the maintenance hatch in the floor.

He remained bent, turning to address Mr. Stone, whose head snapped up to Ari's face guiltily. Ari struggled to remember how to shove words out of his mouth.

"Do. Ahem. Do you have the requisite tools, Mr. Stone? I'm afraid we only have a basic toolkit aboard."

Orin had already turned away, trotting down the open ramp and tossing his words over his shoulder. "Sure do. I'll just fetch my things right quick, be back before you miss me."

Ari shut his mouth against any reply he might have made alluding to whether or not he would miss Mr. Orin Stone.

He settled onto the bench in the main cabin, taking his pad out of his pocket to make an order for sundries, paying the exorbitant fee for same-day delivery from the local ship supply.

Ari was deep into calculations for amounts needed of dehydrated grain when a metallic thud slammed to the floor beside him.

Mr. Stone released the handle of a large metal toolbox that had clearly seen better days, if not decades. It might have been painted red at some point, but any remaining color was now merely an accent to the dented steel case.

Orin straightened, an ancient duffle bag slung over his shoulder. Ari valiantly refrained from noting the way the weight of his luggage caused the muscles in Orin's arm to strain and bulge dramatically. Excessively, even. Practically obscene.

If one were to notice such things, which Ari didn't.

He released a shaky breath as Orin strode down the corridor to toss his bag into Theo's empty room before returning for his toolbox.

"I'll get right to it, professor. Have her fixed up before you know it."

Ari continued to refrain from noticing how the even heavier weight of the toolbox had a similarly obscene effect on the muscles of Mr. Stone's arm and back and...backside.

An obnoxious beeping alert from Ari's pad notified him that he had attempted to order three thousand pounds of dehydrated grain, which exceeded the available supply. That would have been a very unfortunate purchase considering they only needed three pounds.

The clunk of the toolbox settling into the corridor brought his attention back to the pilot who now stood with his hands on his hips, considering the small opening of the maintenance hatch.

Ari set his pad aside to join him in staring at the narrow access.

"Perhaps it would be best if I were to enter, and you could direct me in the repairs?"

Orin's lips curved into a broad smirk, glinting eyes sweeping along the length of Ari's body before peering again into the open panel.

"Oh, don't you worry, Red. I've got a real talent for fitting into tight spaces."

Ari spun around to hide the ridiculous blush on his face as Orin slowly and painstakingly lowered his bulk into the hatch.

Ari finished up his order, switching over to a program his contacts in the Information Technologies department had assured him would prove useful in fabricating documents to get across the Verge, painfully aware that his brother's fate rested in his unsteady hands.

And now, the very steady, very large hands of an unknown pilot.

Chapter Three

Sparks flew, lighting up the corridor amidst the sounds of clanging metal and whirring power tools.

Ari stepped carefully around the open floor hatch, pressing flat against the farthest wall in an attempt to avoid singe marks on his clothing.

He'd just reached the laboratory door when the whirring ended abruptly, accompanied by loud and colorful cursing beneath the floor.

He paused, counting a few silent beats before one final *clang* and a softer yet emphatic continuation of the cursing.

With a longing glance toward his neglected laboratory, Ari doubled back to crouch gingerly near the edge of the open hatch.

"Is everything quite alright?" he inquired, chewing on his lower lip as he awaited a response.

And waited.

And waited.

He opened his mouth to ask again, bracing a hand on the cold metal floor to lean over the hatch, when a head of messy brown hair popped up in front of him, safety goggles shoved haphazardly atop the bony brow.

"I mucked up my hand on the rusted wire stripper. Gotta stop the bleeding so I can get back to repairs."

Orin winced, twisting his face into a comically irritated expression as he gave a sharp exhale before folding his shoulders inward and wedging his bulk out of the hatch one shoulder at a time.

He punctuated his slow progress with dark muttering in a language Ari was grateful he'd never studied, suppressing a sharp pain at the knowledge that Theo would have gleefully interpreted if he'd been present.

Ari's distraction fled as Orin managed to free his elbows and pull himself onto the floor, his left hand leaving smears of blood across the polished steel surface, leaking fast and thick enough to catch and pool around the riveted depressions holding the floor together.

"You're injured!" Ari blurted, reaching out a hand to the pilot who unexpectedly flinched backward before rising to his feet.

"Barely. Just fetch the med kit, would ya, honey?"

Holding his left wrist tightly with the opposite hand, Orin raised it above his head before stomping off toward the galley, scant inches of clearance between his bloody fingertips and the polished ceiling panels.

Ari scrambled to retrieve the med kit he kept stored in his laboratory, still pristine and sealed in plastic wrap from the ship supply.

He found Orin seated at the minuscule dining table, hand still held aloft over a thunderous expression.

Blood dripped down the length of his arm, prompting Ari to drop the med kit to the tabletop, watching Orin expectantly.

Honey-brown eyes caught him in a flat stare for long moments before Orin sighed, lowering his right hand to scrabble against the shrink wrap ineffectually.

Ari grabbed the med kit, stumbling out an apology as he tore the wrapping open and undid the metal latches holding the case of medical supplies closed.

Once he managed to remove the lid, he studied the contents blankly before turning back to Orin.

Orin was examining his injured hand, poking at the deep gash with fingers darkened with machine oil in a most unsanitary manner. Ari grabbed cleansing wipes and seized Orin's hands, dabbing them gently and thoroughly, blood continuing to well up from the wound and drip onto the table.

Orin kept tonguing the side of his mouth thoughtfully; the gesture sending unexplained heat to Ari's cheeks.

"Gonna need stitches, seems like."

Holding his bleeding hand away from the open kit, Orin picked a few items from the assortment, moving bandages and tubes of ointment out of the way to gather the correct supplies.

He held out a sealed needle and packet of surgical thread to Ari, who froze in horror. Orin sighed, waving the packets in Ari's direction.

"Don't worry, sunshine, I can do it myself. I just need you to thread the needle for me."

Nodding, Ari donned the stretchy blue gloves from the dispenser slot at the side of the kit, readied the needle, and handed it back before hesitating.

"Are you certain you wish to stitch up your own hand? Do you have prior experience in suturing a wound?"

Orin rolled his eyes in exasperation, wiggling the hand he had extended to accept the needle impatiently.

"Sure. Been patching myself up long as I can remember. Won't be pretty, but it'll hold." He chuckled darkly. "Not like these big ol' mitts can get much uglier anyway."

Ari frowned, reaching into the kit for a tube of analgesic, adding a dab carefully around the wound. With a deep breath, he leaned in and cradled the injured hand carefully in his much smaller grasp, using his free hand to begin neat, meticulous stitches, tying each off individually before moving on to the next.

"I think your hands are beautiful," Ari muttered, voice trailing off as he realized he'd spoken aloud.

To his horror, the prickling burn of a deep flush immediately covered every visible inch of his skin. He ducked his head, focusing on the wound, painfully aware his skin was burning right under Orin's patrician nose. The curse of his complexion.

As he tied the final suture, Ari braced himself before looking up again, expecting a broad, mocking smirk and surprised to find the pilot smiling softly.

Orin dipped his chin gently at their still-joined hands. "Thank you, professor."

He moved to pull away, but Ari tightened his grip, careful of the fresh stitches.

"Wait. Allow me to apply regeneration fluid first."

Orin's brows climbed up his forehead.

"Nah. No need to waste good regen on me; stuff's expensive."

Ari had already located the correct tube and dispensed a small amount of the fluid onto the wound, carefully ensuring even application.

"I will reapply every six hours until the wound has healed sufficiently."

He hesitated at the stunned expression on Orin's face.

"That is, unless you'd prefer reapplying it yourself?"

Orin shook his head slowly, eyes never leaving Ari's red face.

"No, that's— You can do it. I'll just come to you."

Ari nodded, curling his fingers against the sudden chill as Orin removed his injured hand and snapped a stretched-thin glove over it before standing from the table.

"Best get back to it. Ship's not gonna fix herself."

*

Their evening repast was a quiet affair. Orin ate quickly, hunched over his plate with elbows out.

Ari sat across from him, cutting his food into small bites he could chew discreetly, attempting not to stare at his companion and doing a poor job of it.

Each time Orin lifted his head, Ari lowered his attention to his plate, knowing his skin was as scarlet as his hair.

Orin drew breath to speak, and Ari tensed, waiting to be teased for his inappropriate compliment.

"Where'd you learn a thing like that?"

Ari watched him cautiously, raising his napkin to dab at the corner of his mouth.

"Pardon?"

Orin placed his left hand palm up on the table, displaying the neat row of stitches. The edges of the wound were already beginning to close, aided by the cellular acceleration of the regeneration fluid. Orin gestured at his hand with a jut of his chin.

"Had much experience stitching up a man?"

Ari gave a small smile, shaking his head. "Not men, Mr. Stone. I participated in a series of experiments on mice during my undergraduate studies which required mastery of several surgical techniques."

Orin's mouth kicked up in surprise, amusement coloring his voice. "Mice, huh? I'm glad for it. Mighty nice of you to bother. If I'd have tried it on my own, it would've been a real mess, like this one here."

He pulled his open collar to the side, revealing a jagged scar splitting the smooth bronze skin from collarbone to bulging deltoid on his left side.

Ari's mouth unaccountably went dry before filling with such an excess of saliva it forced him to swallow. Audibly.

The softness faded from Orin's eyes as he kept them trained on Ari's crimson face. He slipped both arms through his leather braces in a practiced motion before reaching behind his neck to grab his shirt with his good hand.

The rustle of fabric slipping over his head seemed to echo in Ari's ears.

Orin dropped his shirt to the floor, pointing to a shorter scar tucked between the ridges of his abdomen. "This one here was the first time I had to stitch myself up. Ugly as sin, right?"

Ari couldn't breathe.

Every inch of the pilot's torso was corded with muscle, moving hypnotically beneath golden bronze skin. A smattering of scars marred the surface, but the unusual sight of them only seemed to enhance his overwhelming masculinity. Dark brown hair dusted the broad muscles of his chest before tapering down into a thick line disappearing beneath the waist of his trousers.

Ari's heartbeat throbbed in his fingertips.

Orin had fallen silent, watching as Ari stared at the expanse of skin for an obscene amount of time.

His throat tightened. Ari had to gasp an awkward breath before garbling out something about the med kit and disappearing down the corridor to fetch it.

He took a moment in his lab to press his burning face against the cool metal of the bulkhead, adjusting his trousers to a more discreet arrangement before returning to the galley.

Orin had restored his shirt, though his braces still hung in loops around his hips. He stood holding Ari's plate, rapidly consuming the remains of Ari's meal.

He seemed genuinely surprised at Aristotle's return, lowering the plate from his face sheepishly. "Alright if I finish this up? Looked like you were done with it."

Ari nodded, resting the med kit on the table in the space where his plate had been.

He sat, willing his hands not to shake as he unlatched the kit, donned a pair of gloves, and located the tube of regeneration fluid.

Orin grabbed the other plate from the table and popped them both in the small galley sonic before taking his customary seat across from Aristotle.

Clutching the tube, Ari forced his fingers to relax enough to reach out for Orin's hand.

The heat of Orin's skin as he rested his hand in Ari's palm transferred swiftly through the glove. Ari looked up as a cleansing wipe was pressed into his other hand, sliding in to nestle against the regen tube.

Orin was watching him carefully, face guarded and dimples hidden.

Ari quickly dropped his focus to his task, gently cleaning the wound before applying a thin layer of fluid. The stitches would disintegrate in another few hours once the regen had done its job.

Orin cleared his throat, nearly startling Ari into dropping the cap he was fumbling back onto the tube.

"You got somebody special waiting on you back home?"

Ari flinched back in his seat, examining the pilot's face for any hint of malice.

"No, there's no one waiting on me, special or otherwise."

Orin's brows twisted skeptically. "No handsome university man crying into his microscope over you?"

The blood left Ari's face, his numb fingers dropping the tube to the table.

"How— How did you know that I—that I have a preference for men?"

Orin appeared, of all things, concerned, holding both hands out palm up in a universal gesture of calming.

"Didn't mean nothing by it. Just saying, I like looking at you, and I see the way you like looking at me. I was just wondering what was holding you back. Thought maybe you had a fella back home or something."

Ari attempted to control his rapid breathing, struggling to remove his gloves.

"I don't."

Orin's dimples reappeared as he replaced the regen in the med kit and latched it shut. He held it out to Ari.

"Well then, you and I could make this trip a hell of a lot more fun, gorgeous."

Ari took the kit, hugging it to his chest. "What do you mean?"

The confident smirk on Orin's face slid downward.

"I meant we could spend some time in my bunk, sweetheart. I don't think I've been exactly subtle."

Ari's eyes widened as it finally sank in, his skin glowing as the rest of his body took immediate, humiliating interest.

"You're sexually attracted to me?"

Orin huffed out a surprised bark of laughter. "Don't think I could have been any more obvious after that striptease. Hell, what did you think all that sweet talk was for?"

Ari's arms tightened around the kit. "I thought you were mocking me."

The light in the pilot's eyes dimmed, mouth drawing straight. "I wouldn't do that."

Ari nodded, tongue heavy and clumsy in his mouth.

"Alright, then."

Orin leaned forward in his seat, lips curving back up at the corners.

"Alright what, honey?"

Ari couldn't meet his gaze, adjusting the kit in his arms self-consciously.

"Alright, yes. Your. Your bunk. We should. That."

The silence grew oppressive as sweat gathered across Ari's forehead, prickling at the base of his spine.

"Nah," Orin said.

Ari snapped his head up, a fresh wave of burning flush sweeping over his skin at the humiliation.

"Oh. Of. Of course. Of course not. I understand why you wouldn't. With me."

The rough edge of Orin's thumb brushed softly across the meat of Ari's lower lip before settling on his chin, lifting Ari's face to his.

"It's not like that. Just saying not tonight, is all. Give me time to prepare. I can pick up some supplies tomorrow morning before we head out."

Ari scrunched his brow in confusion.

"Supplies?"

Orin searched his eyes, a surprised grin spreading across his face, instantly taking years off with a boyish sparkle that reached both dimples.

"You've got no idea, do you, baby? Holy shit, I'm a bad man."

Chapter Four

Ari got very little sleep that night, a fact he would have liked to have attributed entirely to anxiety over the significant risk and high stakes of their upcoming journey. He could confidently say all of that was definitely a factor.

However.

He glared down the length of his body at his tented trousers as though the sheer force of his disapproval could rectify the situation. He was abysmally unsuccessful.

Deciding on the course of ignoring the situation until it improved, he busied himself with organizing the freshly delivered supplies, checking everything off on his pad as he went.

When Orin returned to the ship in the afternoon with a parcel under his arm, Ari ducked into his laboratory, face burning with the effort not to guess at the contents.

When they met at the table to discuss star maps and codes and compare calculations, Ari allowed his tension to melt away under the soothing repetition of mathematics.

Until Orin met his eyes with a slow smile, brushing broad fingertips over his own lips as if trying to wipe it away.

The situation resumed with an intensity bordering on painful.

The only thing that relieved the tension was the gut-wrenching moment when they strapped into their seats as

Ari got his first chance to witness Orin's capabilities as a pilot.

Used to the sensation of turbulence and ominous quaking upon takeoff, Ari could only observe in astonishment as they broke atmo without a tremor.

Orin shot a cheeky wink in his direction, eyes wild but hands steady on the controls.

"Like a hot knife through butter, baby!"

Nothing about that should have exacerbated Ari's situation.

And yet.

He watched Orin pilot the craft with nothing short of exemplary skill as they set a course designed to avoid the notice of any Enforcers patrolling the Verge.

A course that necessitated long stretches of nothing at the slowest pace they could stand.

Ari hung back in the corridor as Orin checked and double-checked the autopilot before declaring them fit for a rest period.

Attempting to appear as though he had business standing there, Ari focused on his pad, tapping the screen every time it went blank from disuse.

Every muscle of his body went rigid as the sound of Orin's footsteps headed in his direction.

Ari stared at the blank screen until his eyes watered as the footsteps slowed, stopped, and then continued into Orin's bunk with a hiss of his door sliding shut.

Ari almost dropped his pad in disappointment.

Instead, he opened his door with a heartfelt sigh and tossed his pad to bounce on the bed. He had just turned to close the door but paused at the hiss of Orin's door sliding open again.

He found honey eyes watching him, crinkled at the edges in a knowing smirk.

"You coming, Red?"

Ari followed Orin into his room like a man sleepwalking, body in motion before his mind could catch up.

He surveyed the bed anxiously, relieved when Orin stopped and turned as soon as his door hissed shut. Relieved until he realized he was stuck between Orin and the bulkhead just behind him, with very little room to move in either direction.

Orin leaned in slightly, resting one hand on the wall over Ari's head. His expression was open and inquisitive, searching Ari's face.

"Ever done this before, beautiful?"

Ari tensed. "Of course I have, don't be ridiculous."

Orin tilted his head, chocolate-brown hair flopping with the motion, making him resemble nothing so much as an overlarge puppy.

"Naw. You're greener than those pretty eyes, darling."

Ari studied the floor, clammy hands clasped behind his back in an effort to curb the trembling.

"Will that be an issue for you?"

He closed his eyes as a large hand grazed over the top of his head, circling around to rest lightly against the nape of his neck. Orin tapped his index finger gently just under Ari's hairline.

"Just means I gotta be a little more thorough, is all. I'll take real good care of you, baby, don't you worry about that. I just gotta ask though. How?"

Ari finally met Orin's warm gaze, steady beneath the dark shaggy fringe of his hair. "How, what, precisely?"

"How'd a pretty thing like you make it all the way to my big paws completely untouched? Doesn't seem possible."

Ari shrugged uncomfortably. "The opportunity has never presented itself. No one has ever been interested in me in such a way before."

Ari neglected to mention he'd never been so lonely before in all of his life, having been used to the constant companionship of his twin. The loneliness left behind after Theo's disappearance kept him up at night. He would not squander the opportunity to press close to another person until the loneliness faded, if only for a few moments.

Orin's grip tightened infinitesimally around Ari's neck.

"Bull. Shit. They weren't interested. I been all over the Core, past the Verge and through the dark and I've never seen a sight as good as you, gorgeous. Hell, I was ready to beat down three pieces of flotsam who were sniffing after you over at the saloon the moment we met."

Ari's face twitched against a smile, attention split between Orin's steady regard and the rosy flush of his full lips. Lips that parted slowly to reveal the edge of a long tongue peeking out to moisten them.

Ari's heart engaged in rigorous calisthenics.

He shook his head slightly, wrenching his focus from Orin's lips. "False flattery is entirely unnecessary. I assure you of my willing participation, regardless."

Orin blinked so slowly Ari thought for a moment he had simply shut his eyes. "Pardon?"

Ari sighed. "I refer to all of this 'sweet talk'"—he lifted both hands to bend his index and middle fingers into air quotes to emphasize his point—"you have been directing at me. I do not require flattery and falsehoods to garner my favor, Mr. Stone."

Mr. Stone frowned, moving a step closer until the heat of him emanated down the length of Ari's body. A heat rivaled only by Ari's resulting blush.

"You calling me a liar, Red?"

Ari shook his head, pressing his hands flat against Orin's chest; it felt like pushing against a wall, having an immediate negative impact on the structural integrity of his knees.

"No. Not as such. I simply. I understand that such words are well intended, but I am also aware of the deficiencies in my physical appearance. You do not need to pretend I am anything other than what I am to gain access to my body, Mr. Stone."

The solid wall beneath his hands rose and fell in an exaggerated deep breath, the exhalation ruffling the hair at the top of Ari's head regardless of his carefully applied pomade.

"Yeah, that's enough of that."

Ari took a sharp breath of his own as the hand that had rested behind his neck circled around to cup his jaw, spanning from ear to ear with thumb and fingertips. Orin's irises were molten bronze.

"Think I already told you to call me Orin, sweetheart. You can also call me lots of other things if you want to, but this Mr. Stone shit stays out of the bedroom, understand?"

Ari nodded as best he could within Orin's grip.

"Good. Now, as for what I'm calling you, you got a choice in that too. You don't like something I'm saying, you tell me. But don't you think for a minute that anything I'm telling you is a lie. I say it how I see it and damn, honey, I don't see nothing but perfection when I look at you."

Ari had to close his eyes against Orin's earnestness.

Orin shifted a little closer, fingers readjusting on Ari's jaw, the thick edge of his thumb sweeping back against one earlobe.

"That's alright, sugar, we'll work on that. We got all the time we need and nobody around to interrupt."

Ari couldn't suppress the shiver that started in his fingertips and ran a course through his entire body until his lower lip trembled against the webbing between Orin's forefinger and thumb. He kept his eyes shut tight as he attempted to will it away.

Orin lowered his head to drift his lips down Ari's hairline to his ear, making gentle shushing noises as he circled Ari's waist with his other hand. He walked them backward a couple of steps until the cool panels of the bulkhead supported his back.

The hand around his jaw turned his head up and to the side, everything pausing for a breathless moment until he lifted his lashes to find Orin studying his face like he had all the patience in the galaxy.

"Yeah?"

Ari felt the question more than he heard it, Orin's voice soft and deep within the rumble of his chest, standing close enough that they pressed together with every breath.

Ari swallowed, Orin's hand stroking gently down his throat as though chasing the motion. "Yeah. Yes," he whispered.

The heat of Orin's lips hit Ari's senses before the weight of them. Ari froze for a second, body tensing until he realized that Orin had paused, just like that. Lips a subtle pressure against Ari's own, large hands rubbing tiny circles up and down Ari's back and arms.

Ari relaxed in increments. First, his fingers released from fists to curl tentatively around Orin's heavy biceps, then his neck released to lean his head back against the metal panel, followed by a slow unraveling of his entire body.

It felt a little like he imagined a solid mineral might upon reaching the melting point, were such a mineral to have somehow achieved sentience.

Orin seemed to have been waiting for Ari to relax, the release of tension sending him into motion.

He dragged his lips slowly across Ari's before taking his lower lip between his own and sucking gently. Ari gasped and Orin's tongue slid inside his mouth, just barely meeting Ari's tongue.

The sensation was electric, shooting all the way down directly to his cock. Ari made a noise in his throat as his hips jerked without his intention. Orin crowded closer, lowering one hand to grasp Ari's hip as the other rose to hold the back of his head, providing a cushion between Ari's skull and the bulkhead. He pulled back his head, brushing their lips together a few times before trailing his lips down Ari's jawline to his ear.

"That's it, beautiful, just like that."

Ari keened, Orin's deep voice and soft words sending a rush of warmth through his entire body. Orin nodded against his neck, grazing the edge of his teeth over Ari's skin.

"Knew you'd be sweet just like this. Already so good for me, baby."

Ari moved his hands from where they had been clawing Orin's biceps to coast over the wide crest of his shoulders, leaving one there as he tentatively explored the span of his back with the other, enjoying the muscles rolling under his hands. Orin huffed quietly as Ari slid his hand under the open hem of his shirt, fingertips barely brave enough to make contact with his skin.

"Good. That's good, gorgeous. Love it when you touch me."

Ari nodded mindlessly as the words lifted him higher and higher, growing braver with his hand on Orin's back, rolling his palm into the firm skin as he dug in with his fingertips.

Orin slid his thigh between Ari's legs, pressing even closer together until he rubbed against Ari's throbbing cock. Ari tried to swallow a moan as he shifted restlessly beneath the answering length of Orin's cock pressed hard against his abdomen.

Orin returned to his lips, less controlled than before, his movements firmer and more insistent. Ari opened to him, thrilling at the reintroduction of their tongues. He tentatively followed Orin's as it left his mouth, tracing the pillowy inner flesh of Orin's bottom lip with the pointed tip of his tongue.

Orin groaned into Ari's mouth, the sound of it rumbling down his throat. Ari grasped at Orin with both hands, sliding the one at his shoulder into the open collar of his shirt, seeking skin. His fingertips eagerly explored the contrast between the silk of Orin's skin and the rougher texture of his scars.

Orin pulled back to watch him, the amber of his iris nearly swallowed by the dark of his pupil until it was just a halo of gold. Ari panted, attempting to lift his head to follow, but the hand supporting the back of his skull held him in place, broad fingertips scratching gently through his hair. Orin licked his lips, chest heaving with his breath.

"Look at you. Never seen something so good, baby, I swear."

Ari surged forward, mashing his lips inexpertly on Orin's until Orin grunted quietly, reclaiming control of the kiss with gentle lips, his hand guiding Ari's movements at the base of his skull.

Something rose within Ari, something wild and uncontrolled. The notion should have terrified him, but he felt nothing but safe in Orin's arms, sheltered beneath the bulk of his body.

Ari moved his hand from Orin's shoulder to shove his shirttails out of the way and glide over the ridges of Orin's abdomen. Orin tensed as Ari traced the top edge of the belt riding low on his hips and slid slender fingertips just beneath the buckle. A feral sound growled from Orin's throat as he shifted his grip on Ari's hip, long fingers reaching back until he cupped his ass, squeezing slowly. Ari made a noise that should have been embarrassing, but he couldn't bring himself to care.

Orin tilted Ari's hips, pulling until Ari was rocking into the solid length of Orin's thigh. Ari gasped, fingers digging into Orin's flesh as lightning surged down his spine.

Orin spoke directly into his mouth, words traveling from his tongue to Ari's. "Perfect. So perfect for me."

He sucked on the tip of Ari's tongue just as he rocked forward with his thigh, and Ari cried out sharply, hips moving uncontrollably as he spilled into his trousers. The sudden euphoria set his entire body to shaking under Orin's hands.

Orin pulled back, a smile curving his swollen lips. "Did you just—"

Ari shoved him away, the surprise of it moving Orin's body far more than Ari's meager strength. Orin lifted his hands to hold his palms out to Ari, moving slowly and speaking quietly as though he were gentling a frightened animal.

"Hey, now. It's okay, you're okay, gorgeous."

Ari shook his head, face burning at the mortification. He shouldered past Orin roughly, fumbling at the door controls before stumbling down the corridor to slam his hand against the entry panel to his doorway, tensing in anticipation of the sound of heavy footsteps that never came as he escaped into the solitude of his bunk.

Chapter Five

The soft light of simulated dawn crept across Aristotle's ceiling panels with an unrelenting cheer he found most unwelcome.

Ducking his head beneath the covers, Ari groaned.

This was going to be miserable. There was a reason he'd spent his entire life alone with the exception of his twin. Many reasons actually. The previous night's experience encapsulated several of them quite succinctly.

Aristotle was a man of many talents, none of which included fraternization. He was simply ill-suited for the company of others. He was apparently especially ill-suited for the company of devastatingly attractive Verge pilots. He was especially, *particularly* ill-suited for engaging in romantic assignations with said pilot.

His stomach churned at the knowledge that he would be forced to work in close quarters with Orin as soon as he exited his bunk. He might even be required to engage in conversation or, heavens forbid, eye contact.

The very notion made Ari contemplate the heretofore unappealing option of opening the bay doors and flinging himself into the frozen vacuum of space.

A muffled sound from the main cabin prompted Ari to drag himself into his minuscule sonic, turning it up far too high until he felt battered by the cleansing waves. His third shower since last night, which Ari chose to consider thorough, rather than excessive. He was similarly thorough in applying his pomade, his comb ruthless in its command of every strand of distressingly vibrant hair.

Ari then spent far too long making his bed with flattened sheets and precisely folded corners before dressing himself in as many layers as he could manage. Undershirt and drawers, stockings with garters, shirtsleeves, starched collar and cuffs, trousers, waistcoat, cravat, jacket, spats. Every seam perfectly straight and every button done up and centered, Ari ran out of reasons to delay.

Refusing to acknowledge any incidental resemblance to a recently caught fish gasping upon the deck, Ari took several deep breaths before carefully placing his hand on the panel to open the door. He peered out into the corridor, spats creaking at the odd angle he had to assume in order to assure that he exposed nothing past his eyes.

Nothing.

The corridor was empty, no movement in the main cabin. The doors to Orin's bunk, the laboratory, and the cockpit were all closed.

Ari turned his face into the cuff of his jacket to muffle his sigh of relief.

Putting steel in his posture, he walked out to the galley for a small breakfast of dehydrated protein and grain with a sprinkling of dried fruit on top to make it palatable.

He heard nothing from either end of the ship until he stood to clear his dishes.

The door to the cockpit slid open to reveal Orin appearing bright and well rested, with a hint of dark stubble darkening his jaw. He brightened even further as he caught sight of Ari where he stood frozen in the galley.

The universe, Ari decided, was unfair.

Orin strolled over, Ari's attention snagging on his long fingers as they brushed against the outside of his thighs with every step.

Unfair.

Orin lowered his head to catch his gaze.

"Morning, gorgeous."

Ari turned away, loading the sonic with unnecessary concentration.

Orin grazed his fingertips down Ari's sleeve, but Ari pulled away, steeling himself to meet Orin's eyes.

Orin's expression was open and gentle, a small smile curving the line of his mouth.

"You don't need to be embarrassed, sweetheart, watching you come apart like that was just about the hottest thing I've ever seen. Surprised you didn't melt a hole in the wall, you burned so bright for me."

Ari shook his head, raising his chin against the urge to let it hang in shame.

"It was an experiment. A failed experiment. I won't subject you to my inexpert attentions again."

Orin tilted his head, the hand that had reached for Ari combing back through his messy hair in a gesture Ari might have called nervous on anyone else.

"Isn't an experiment meant to be repeated? Over and over and over again? That's just good science, professor."

His eyes crinkled at the corners, the tip of his tongue poking out teasingly between his teeth.

Expecting ridicule, Ari was thrown off course by this gentle teasing and reassurance. The steel he had so carefully and painfully injected into his spine was distressingly susceptible to the melting sensation he had discovered in Orin's arms just hours before.

Ari wanted nothing more than to melt just like Orin had said, until they burned a hole through the wall, until they burned a hole through the entire ship. It would be so easy to forget his worries in Orin's arms.

The truth of that thought finally strengthened his resolve, and he squared his shoulders as he faced Orin head on.

"It was rash of me. My brother's life hinges upon my success, and I cannot afford such a meaningless diversion."

Orin nodded as he faced the floor, thumb rubbing hard across his lower lip. When he looked back up at Ari, the hint of softness had fled his gaze.

"Meaningless diversion. Gotcha. Well, there's no need to worry about me bothering you, I ain't one to hang around when I'm not wanted."

Ari's throat closed around the urge to explain that it was never a question of wanting.

That he felt as though he could drown in the wanting.

That it was the overwhelming depth of the wanting that posed the problem.

Orin had already turned away, sauntering off to his bunk with a lazy grace Aristotle could only marvel at.

Ari made his way to the cockpit, where he settled into the copilot's seat and activated the holopad on his side of the view screen to transfer data from his personal pad for closer review.

He pulled up the nonsensical scribblings Theo had left on the back of the note that had stopped Ari's heart.

Lists of unrelated words, phonetically spelled as Theo did when discerning accents and dialects. Incomplete sketches of geometrical designs: three interlocking triangles, a labyrinthine river of parallel straight lines intersected with tiny circles, and small hexagonal shapes nestled close together.

Hangul characters, messily scrawled in imperfect rows down the margins on each side.

Ari had yet to make heads or tails of it.

He jerked in his seat, closing his notes as the door hissed open and Orin walked in. He unceremoniously dropped into the pilot's seat and fired up his own holopad, activating the view screen as he switched out of autopilot. Ari sat silently and watched the projections light up across the clear simulated quartz, informing them of their speed, location, and state of the ship.

Orin didn't glance up from the screen, fingers dancing over his controls as he spoke. He hadn't shaved, the shadows on his face bringing his cheekbones into sharp relief.

Unfair.

"Making our first stop in a few minutes. I know a place, small settlement but honest folk. They won't cheat us any more than they have to."

Ari leaned back in affront.

"Why would you frequent an establishment that you know will 'cheat you'?"

Orin's eyes were hard as they skated over Ari's face and back to the controls.

"People gotta eat, professor. Things can get mighty scarce out here. Everyone on the Verge knows the score."

They operated in silence as Orin pulled up to the settlement, which appeared little more than a rock through the view screen.

Their landing was just as astoundingly smooth as their takeoff had been, the largest difference being Orin's continued silence as he guided them into the tiny dock.

Ari felt like he was holding his breath, both of them watching the controls as Orin shut down the ship, locking it in place.

As soon as he finished, Orin turned with a smirk on his face.

"Well, professor, you wanna get ready to go?"

Ari unbuckled his harness and straightened his jacket as he stood.

"I'm ready."

Orin gaped at him before breaking into an inexplicable fit of laughter.

He laughed so hard he would have fallen out of his chair if it weren't for his harness, broad chest shaking as he wiped tears away.

"Oh, no you ain't, Red. People round here'll take one look at you and charge us triple. You got anything a little less—" He considered the emerald velvet lapel of Ari's jacket critically.

Ari threw one hand up in exasperation. "A little less what, precisely?"

Orin raked him over from the polished black tips of Ari's shoes up to the delicate lace of his cravat.

"Just, a little. Less. Something without all that pretty nonsense you like to wrap yourself in like you're a little gift. There's men out here that would see all those fripperies as an invitation."

Ari peered down at himself, smoothing his hands over his embroidered waistcoat. "An invitation to what? Larceny?"

Orin rolled his shoulders as he turned away, muscle jumping in his jaw. "If you're lucky."

Ari opened his mouth to inquire further, but Orin unbuckled his harness, running a hand through his hair with a sigh as he glanced at Ari.

"Look, just take my word for it. Don't you have something to wear for getting your hands dirty? Anything at all? I'd offer my second shirt, but you'd be as lost as a flea on an elephant's ass in it."

Ari considered his limited travel wardrobe, which contained slight variations of everything he was wearing. He met Orin's eyes and shook his head, pulling on his cuff self-consciously

"No, I. I don't. This is just how I dress. It has never been an issue before."

Orin's face softened, his hand making an aborted motion toward Ari's arm before falling into a loose fist at his side.

"And you're beautiful just as you are, honey, I'm just trying to keep you safe. Pretty thing like you is liable to get eaten up out here, and not in a good way."

Ari crinkled his nose, mouthing *good way* behind Orin's back as he slid past him to walk out into the main cabin.

Orin leaned against the galley cabinets, arms folded over his chest. The manner in which his pose caused his biceps to swell made a thin sheen of sweat break out on Ari's scalp. He scanned Ari up and down again, something Aristotle was shocked to discover he was getting increasingly accustomed to. Orin tilted his head.

"Lose the jacket."

Ari complied, folding it neatly and placing it on the table.

Orin nodded thoughtfully. "And the vest. And the neck...thing."

Ari rolled his eyes as he slid the buttons free on his waistcoat; he then lay it atop his jacket before moving to work on the complicated knot at his neck.

"It is called a cravat."

Orin hummed an acknowledgement and bobbed his head distractedly, attention glued to Ari's fingers at his throat as he unwrapped the length of fabric before folding and placing it atop his waistcoat. The way Orin stared at the exposed line of his throat made Ari acutely aware he was standing there in his shirtsleeves, barely decent. He swallowed and looked away, resisting the urge to cover his neck with his hand.

Orin pushed off of the cabinets and approached close enough to take a pinch of Ari's sleeve between his fingers.

"Never seen something so fine."

While clearly referencing the shirt, Orin's focus remained stuck on Ari's face, gliding down to his exposed throat as Ari swallowed once again.

Ari took a halting breath. "Will I pass muster, Mr. Stone?"

They both reacted to the name, a sudden flash of heat crossing Orin's face as Ari's eyes dropped to his lips, remembering his admonishment on using his surname in the bedroom. But they weren't in a bedroom, they were in the main cabin, Ari attempting to calm the odd feeling rising up his spine at the thought. It was like panic, but sweeter somehow.

Orin stepped backward, rubbing his fingers lightly over his lips as he gave Ari a once-over. Ari wished he wouldn't, it was difficult enough to stop thinking about them without the encouragement.

Orin nodded slowly in approval. "Think you'll do just fine for now. We'll get you turned out nice and proper when we get there."

Chapter Six

Ari peered around the settlement as they walked from the docks. The sky had an artificial blue-green tinge that only came from manufactured atmosphere, the air leaving a metallic aftertaste with every breath. Deserted dirt roads spread out in cardinal directions, flanked by squat buildings. The entire town appeared to have been constructed from debris.

One building sported a fraction of a woman's painted face on a large wooden fragment of some advertisement, patched together with metal and wooden planks of every color and size. The next building was a variation on the same theme, the small overhang covering the front porch supported by mismatched copper pipes.

Aristotle had never seen anything like it.

Orin slowed as they approached a building trimmed by a raised porch equipped with rocking chairs. A fresh coat of whitewash minimized the uneven surface of the mixed planks forming the exterior walls.

A creaking wooden sign swung in the breeze, cheerfully painted with Sally's Sundries at a charming slant.

Orin's boots rattled the spindly metal banister as he tromped up the front steps, Ari following close behind.

The front door, cut from a chunk of perforated metal ship flooring, clanged shut behind them loudly, letting sunlight stream in a dotted pattern across the concrete floor.

A young woman puttered about behind the counter, wrapping a parcel with twine to be stacked with others off to the side. She appeared tired in the way Ari had noticed seemed to fall on all Verge women, but she was clean and pretty nonetheless. It was simply that the lines on her face didn't match the age in her eyes. Her ill-fitting dress threatened to fall off one shoulder as she worked, the faded floral fabric cinched in at the waist with a man's thick leather belt, which sported, of all things, a holstered pistol.

Ari made his best effort not to stare at it.

Orin sauntered up to the counter with his thumbs in his leather braces.

"Hey there, sugar! You surely are a sight for sore eyes!"

The woman lifted her head, the smile on her face revealing her youth.

"Why, if it isn't Orin Stone himself! I haven't seen you in a dog's age!"

Orin tucked his chin to flirt up at her through his lashes, dimples on display. "And I been pining away for you all this time, Sally, honest truth."

Sally blinked dazedly, no more immune to Orin's relentless charm than the next poor soul, Ari noted wryly.

She leaned her chin on her hand, bony elbow planted on the counter between them, the tattered lace cuff of her dress splayed out over the surface.

"What brings you back to my humble establishment?"

Orin traced the fabric on the countertop, swirling his finger gently over the lace.

"Maybe I just wanted to see your pretty face again, Sal."

Her eyes narrowed as she pulled her arm away, batting Orin's hand off her cuff, lips curled in to suppress her smile.

"Been a long time, but you're still shoveling the same shit, Stone. Why don't you just go on and tell me what you need so I can get you out of my hair?"

Orin's face lit up as he nodded slowly.

"Alright, alright, I gotcha. Sally Mudd is off the market. When'd you find a man to settle down with, Sal?"

The light wash of pink on her cheeks revealed a flash of the way she could have been, primped and pretty beneath a parasol back on Britannia. She patted her hair shyly, tucking mouse-brown strands back into the loose roll at the nape of her neck.

"'Bout two years back now."

Orin leaned in, one hand resting on his holster, face drawn into a forbidding scowl. "Nice fella? He treat you right?"

She threw back her head with a tinkling laugh, slapping the solid arm Orin kept by his holster hard enough that Ari flinched.

"No call for all that bluster, he treats me just fine."

Orin's scowl melted into a wide grin. "Good to hear. Listen, darlin', I got a new ship on my hands, pretty little explorer vessel, barely opened up, never even had a real pilot at the controls. I'm wanting to do her up right, all the bells and whistles you got. I'm talking premium fuel crystals, the works."

Sally pursed her lips in a long, low whistle.

"The royal treatment, huh? Sounds like you're in love already."

Orin's face stayed turned toward Sally, but Ari saw his gaze flick in Ari's direction from the corner of his eye. His grin tilted up at one end as Ari blushed and turned hastily away.

"Something like that. We're still getting to know each other; she's a shy little thing."

Sally nodded like that made any kind of sense.

"I'll get her fixed up proper, don't you worry, hon. Anything else?"

Orin nodded, tipping his head back in Ari's direction.

"Red needs new duds. Got anything in his size?"

Ari stiffened as they both studied him, Sally's eyes traveling over him in the same way Orin's often did. He surreptitiously considered Orin's eyes, dark in the shadow of his browbone as his teeth pulled at the corner of his bottom lip, making Ari fidget.

Well, not precisely in the same way.

Sally nodded decisively, gesturing Ari closer with a broad motion of her arm.

"I bet I do. Come on, sugar. Let's get you fixed up too."

Ari followed her back through a faded yellow curtain behind the counter as Orin made a shooing motion with his fingers.

Sally bustled around the small stockroom, pulling down boxes here and there and laying them out on a rickety table in the center of the room.

She squinted at Ari's shoulders before putting one box back and pulling another, dropping it on the table with a wink.

"Alright, here's all I got. Give it a try, and come out when you're decent."

She breezed out through the curtain before Ari could reply, left alone with the muffled sound of her continued conversation with Orin and the boom of his answering laugh.

Ari turned reluctantly to the boxes, opening one with trepidation.

He was relieved to find the shirt clean and pressed. It was unbleached ecru linen with odd striations of darker and lighter fibers, collarless in the style favored by Orin. Ari mused that perhaps this style was *au courant* on the Verge.

He checked around before stripping down to his undergarments, then slipped the shirt over his head. It was a decent fit, if a tad more billowy than he would have favored. The other boxes contained close-fitting brown canvas trousers, a double-breasted waistcoat of the same fabric, and brown leather boots that laced to the knee with copper eyelets.

Ari still felt exposed without a collar or cravat and walked out from behind the curtain with one hand hovering over the hollow of his throat.

Sally and Orin both turned to watch him, something unpleasant swooping in his belly at the way she rested her hand on Orin's arm like it belonged there.

Ari cleared his throat. "I believe these garments will prove sufficient."

Sally's peel of surprised laughter struggled out from behind the fingers she clamped over her mouth as soon as Ari opened his.

Orin nudged her shoulder, echoing amusement sketched across his face.

That swooping feeling in Ari's gut began to thicken and solidify until he felt like he had swallowed rocks. He stared down at the toe of his boots, hand fluttering between covering his throat and his mouth.

Sally stepped closer, laughter fading away. "I'm sorry, it's just, we don't get many folks round here that talk like you. Sound like some kinda fairytale prince, don't you, hon?"

Ari had no response to that, stiffening as she approached.

She studied him up and down with one hand on her hip, then twirled the index finger of her other hand in the air over her head.

"Give us a spin; let me take a gander at you."

Ari turned slowly, face burning with a flush creeping over the back of his neck as he sensed their scrutiny on his back.

He tilted his head over his shoulder at Sally surveying the lines of the waistcoat across his back. Orin's gaze had fallen lower, darting away and drifting to the ceiling when Ari caught him, hands stuffed in his trouser pockets.

Sally bustled past Ari, slipped behind the curtain, and emerged almost immediately with something the color of rust dangling from her fingers.

She approached Ari like an old friend, reaching up to loop it over the back of his head and then tying a simple knot at the base of his throat with a decisive nod.

"There you go, sugar. An ascot oughta make you a little more comfortable."

Ari reached up to finger the knot, shoulders relaxing even though it exposed far more of his throat than would have been appropriate back home. He finally felt dressed, at least.

He turned to Orin, who was still chewing on his lip, eyes roaming Ari from the mussed top of his head to the thick heel of his boots.

Ari startled as Sally's thin fingers began to work on the buttons of his waistcoat, sending him stumbling backward in shock.

"I. I don't. What do you think you are doing?"

She lifted her hands, stepping away with a soft laugh. "Just need your vest to make some alterations, show off that trim little waist of yours the way it deserves."

Sally peered over Ari's shoulder at Orin. "Why don't you head on to the docks? I'll send my man down to get you fixed up while I help out your sweetie here."

"I beg your pardon?" Ari sputtered. "I am not his—"

Orin walked over and opened the door, throwing his words over his shoulder. "Sounds good, Sal. Red'll pick up the bill."

The door clanging shut behind him seemed to ring across the space as Ari was left staring at Sally, who drew near with a serene smile, holding out her hand expectantly.

"Vest, please."

Ari went to work on the copper-rimmed buttons and passed the waistcoat over without meeting Sally's eye.

She took it behind the counter, then bent to rummage through something that sounded like a metal box full of other, smaller metal boxes, raising her voice to carry over the sound.

"Y'all haven't been together for long, then?"

Ari approached the counter, arms crossed over his chest, feeling altogether far too exposed.

"I'm afraid you appear to be laboring under a misapprehension, Miss Mudd."

Sally's head popped up, strands of hair escaping from her roll at an alarming rate, waistcoat draped over a small metal box in her arms.

She plopped the box on the counter. After turning the waistcoat wrong-side out, she pulled a needle from the box and considered her limited thread selection. She tilted her head before plucking a card wrapped in a length of brown thread with a satisfied nod.

Sally peeked up at Ari after threading the needle, eyes dancing. "I could just listen at you all day, you sound that pretty."

She lay the needle on top of the waistcoat, turned to lift an ancient pad from the counter, and held it over her head in both hands before bringing it down on the counter with a bang. Then, she repeated the procedure twice more before the screen blinked to life, and proceeded to tap her fingers rapidly across.

She tossed it to the side when she was done, returning to her needle and focusing on a seam.

"There now, Jeb'll have your ship fixed up in no time at all. I believe you were about to tell me all about how you started up with Orin Stone, weren't you, hon?"

Ari tore his attention away from the battered pad, projections still blinking in and out across the cracked screen.

He regarded the top of Sally's head, clearing his throat.

"Mr. Stone and I have recently entered into a partnership in an exploratory venture."

Sally's grin started in her eyes as they flicked up at Ari, spreading across her cheeks before lifting the corners of her mouth. "That what they're calling it up in the Core, nowadays?"

Ari bristled, straightening his shirt cuffs with small, sharp movements. "It is purely a business venture, I assure you."

To call the expression on Sally's face skeptical would have been to call the expanse of the deep dark "big."

She snorted daintily, fingers flying across the seam of the waistcoat. "I'm sorry; I know it's none of mine, but you're just his type, is all." She graced him with a restrained smirk. "And don't try and tell me he ain't yours. I gave you that ascot to mop up the drool."

Ari wished he had a better response to that than an inarticulate squawk.

She picked up the waistcoat to nip the end of the thread off with her teeth, then carefully removed the remaining thread from the needle and wrapped it back around the card before dropping both into the box.

Holding the waistcoat out over the counter, she flapped it in Ari's direction. "There now, oughta fit like a dream."

Ari took it from her and shrugged into and buttoned it as quickly as he could without meeting her eyes, wholly unaccustomed to dressing in front of others.

By the time he finished, she was pushing back through the curtain, Ari's clothing bundled in her arms.

Dropping the lot onto the counter, she whistled at Ari just as Orin had whistled at his ship. "What'd I say? Just like a dream."

Ari blushed under her open observation.

She shook her head as she folded Ari's shirt, then bundled it in brown paper and tied the package with rough twine.

"Orin was right, you are a shy little thing, aren't you?"

Ari's mouth hung open disconcertedly.

"I'm not. He didn't. That was in reference to the ship, Miss Mudd."

Sally peered up at him through sparse brown lashes as she boxed up his spats.

"Sure it was, hon. Now, how'd you like to pay—Ident or Chip?"

Chapter Seven

Sally led the way out onto the porch, Ari following close behind, loaded down with several boxes and parcels, all tied neatly together with twine.

He had secured his personal effects from the pockets of his old waistcoat and trousers and slipped them into the new, slowly growing accustomed to his Verge-style clothing.

It was by turns more and less restrictive than he was used to, and it was already having an effect on his posture and gait.

He surveyed the topography for likely sources, spying a patch of variegated soil that could be the match he was searching for.

Shifting his packages to one arm, Ari stooped to gather a soil sample. He capped the vial and carefully labeled it before sliding it into one of the convenient flap pockets on either side of his new trousers.

They walked past a few more buildings before he stopped to retrieve some sedimentary rocks, then bagged and labeled them before dropping them into the opposite pocket.

Sally stopped to watch him with a furrowed brow.

"I'm sorry, but what the heck are you doing?"

Ari turned away from the empty vial in his hand, granting her a fraction of his attention.

"I am collecting samples."

Sally's mask of confusion blossomed into a mask of continued, deeper confusion.

"What's that supposed to mean?"

Ari swept a dusting of mineral powder into the vial, capped and labeled it, and rose to his feet.

"It means I am gathering geological samples from every Verge settlement I encounter, in order to analyze said samples in my laboratory."

Sally's confusion grew a third layer. "What for?"

Ari brushed the soil from the knees of his trousers, marveling at the ease with which it came away. There was certainly something to be said for Verge clothing when it came to fieldwork. He glanced at Sally as he shifted the parcels in his arms.

"In the desperate hope of saving someone's life," he answered quietly.

The confusion melted from her face, leaving gentle commiseration behind.

He cleared his throat against the threat of a rising lump, blinking sudden moisture away, grasping for a distraction. "Earlier, when you said I was Mr. Stone's type. What, precisely, did you mean by that? Purely out of idle curiosity, of course."

She patted his arm gently before lifting both hands to her face to begin ticking off fingers.

"Well, let's see. You're pretty as a picture, kinda delicate in the way that always draws him in like flies on honey. Sweet, too, I'd wager. Obviously got some brains in your head, and, most importantly, you can't take your eyes off him any more'n he can take his off you."

Aristotle tugged at his ascot, fumbling his parcels as they nearly slid out of his arms.

"Would you. Would you say that Mr. Stone expects a certain level of sophistication, in a partner?"

Sally cut her eyes to his with a twinkle. "Speakin' in terms of business, right, hon?"

Ari nodded stiffly, paper crunching as he held his parcels tightly. "In terms of business, of course."

Sally bobbed her head thoughtfully from side to side. "Naw. Think that man's got more than enough sophistication for the both of you. In terms of business, mind."

Aristotle turned away as heat prickled up his neck, deeply regretting initiating this conversation. "Thank you for your insight, Miss Mudd."

Sally startled him with a light slap on the arm. "Anyone'd be lucky to have you. Why, I'd like to take you home with me just to listen to you talk. Only, Jeb might get a little bent out of shape if I did. As if he don't know he's the only man for me."

She offered him a saucy wink as she slid her hand into the crook of his arm as if they had known each other all their lives, the dust ruffle on her skirts brushing against his boots with every step.

She tugged on his arm just as they drew in sight of the docks, bringing them both to a stop. Ari pivoted to her curiously, finding a serious expression stamped across her face. She pulled until he leaned down close enough to hear as she lowered her voice.

"Listen here, sugar. I'm gonna be the one to tell you this just cause there ain't no one else out there to say it. That Orin Stone is a good man. I know he comes over real rough and tough, but he can't help it if he got size enough for two fellas. Truth is, he's a real sweetie pie, and you'd best not be messing him around or you'll have to answer to Sally Mudd, you hear me? You ask around, and you won't find nobody who'd want to be in your fancy shoes then."

Ari nodded warily as he slowly straightened away from her sharp glare.

It would be fair to say he was dragged the first couple of steps as she resumed her jaunty walk right up to where Ari's ship was docked.

Orin and another man stood at the bottom of the ramp, shirtsleeves rolled up and surrounded by crates they were unloading from a nearby hover wagon.

The other man was tall and handsome, mocha-brown skin contrasting nicely with his tightly curled blond hair. Or, he would have been handsome were it not for the deep trench of scar tissue dragging his skin down from the wide bridge of his nose up into his scalp on the left side. His mismatched eyes focused on Aristotle with a barely audible mechanical whir, soft brown on one side and glowing red on the other.

Orin gestured to him with a toss of his head. "This's Jeb. He's helping get Delilah gussied up for the ball."

Ari couldn't decide which part of the statement was the most confusing.

He opened his mouth to reply, realized there was no reply to be found, and shut his mouth again.

Jeb offered a wave with a sharp flick of his wrist above his head, and Ari raised his hand to wiggle his fingers slightly in response. Orin watched the exchange with good humor before turning away to haul crates of fuel crystals into the open hatch of the exterior storage panels.

Ari turned to Sally. "May I inquire—who is Delilah?"

Sally picked up her skirts to follow Jeb up the ramp, exposing well-worn ankle boots just below the leather sheath of a knife strapped to her embroidered stocking. She threw an unconcerned glance back at Ari. "Beats me, sugar."

Ari followed dazedly, hugging the wall to avoid the open storage and maintenance hatches as he retreated to his bunk to unload his parcels. He carefully unpacked and hung his clothing, making sure all the wall panels were neatly shut before moving to the lab to store his samples.

He emerged to find Jeb closing the maintenance hatch.

Jeb touched his thumb and forefinger to his hairline as if tipping a hat that wasn't there, giving a slight bob of his head in Ari's direction.

"Doctor," he said quietly, voice unexpectedly soft and melodic.

Ari responded with an abbreviated bow. "Mr. Jeb."

Ari suppressed a wince at his own stiff formality as Jeb broke out in a smile before joining Sally at the table. She had a pad out in front of her, an older model but still in much better condition than the one from the store. She beckoned Ari over with a sharp whistle.

"Lookie here, hon. Your man caught my Jeb up on y'all's plans. Noble of you to go chasing after your wayward brother, I gotta say. If it were my rotten sister, I'd leave her to stew in her own pot, and that's a fact."

Jeb snorted in the seat across from Sally as Sally scooted over on the bench, patting the space beside her in a way that should have been enticing but veered all the way into commanding.

Ari gingerly took a seat, surreptitiously pushing Sally's skirts aside as they scandalously spilled over his thigh. She noticed his fidgeting and gathered the fabric in a bundle before shoving it behind her on the bench, exposing her ruffled pantaloons.

Ari genuinely did not know how to react. Sally solved his dilemma with a sharp elbow to his side as she waved the pad in his face.

"Pay attention now. Our fellas've been putting their heads together on this, and now we got y'all a guide. It's not much, but it's something to go on."

Ari turned his attention to the pad she shoved into his hands, carefully manipulating the projections in front of him.

Sally wedged her hand under his to scatter the projections here and there, having obviously grown frustrated with his pace. She pointed out a grid composed of names, locations, and numbers.

"Now, this here's a list of all the best-known singers on the Verge. Least, we got a list of what they go by, where they usually slink around, and the goin' rate for a song."

Ari shook his head, a headache starting just behind his eyes that made him nostalgic for his brother, who was usually the cause. "I'm terribly sorry, Miss Mudd, I'm afraid I don't quite follow. Why would we require the services of a vocalist?"

Jeb gave a quiet huff, bringing both of their attention across the table.

"She's talking about informants. Colloquially known as singers, their information is referred to as a song."

Sally leaned her chin onto her hand with a deep sigh, batting her lashes across the table. "Ooh, Jeb, you know I love it when you bust out your Academy voice."

Ari perked up at the mention of academia, leaning forward slightly. "Where did you attend?"

Jeb stared down at the table, eye focusing with a faint whir. "Enforcer Academy, years back."

Aristotle stiffened, silently considering the open exit ramp. Jeb laughed softly, returning his gaze to Ari's face.

"Relax, Doctor. They kicked my ass out."

Ari tried to nod consolingly when, really, he just wanted to sink with relief. The last thing he needed was an encounter with the Enforcers.

Orin's boots on the loading ramp announced his presence before he entered the cabin, the space suddenly seeming far too small for four people. Ari absolutely did not notice the way his sweat-damp clothing clung to his body. If he had noticed such things, he would have also noted that he'd opened his shirt by two more buttons.

Fortunately, Ari noticed none of these things before snapping his eyes back to the pad Sally took from his suddenly numb fingers with a snicker.

Orin stopped right at the top, one foot planted on the floor while the other disappeared down the ramp. He leaned his elbow on his bent knee.

"Ready for the fun part, Jeb?"

Jeb stood with a chuckle, going to a large crate taking up one side of the floor next to the open ramp. He placed his hand on the lock panel, waiting for the scan to complete before the lid popped open with a quiet beep.

Ari also went to his feet as Sally planted her hands in the small of his back and pushed. He stumbled over to peer into the crate, rearing back as he registered the contents, nearly knocking into Sally behind him.

"Those are—"

Jeb swept one open hand over the top of the crate. "Yup. Welcome to our local armory."

He picked up a midsize ray gun and flipped it over in his hands with a nonchalance Ari found completely unwarranted.

Orin studied the crate for a long moment before selecting a laser pistol nearly the length of Aristotle's forearm and expertly twirling it around his index finger.

Perhaps that particular display was somewhat warranted.

Parts of Ari could definitely stand to see more, in fact.

Ari swallowed discreetly as Orin took aim at the wall, arm fully extended, before repeating the twirl in reverse and tucking the pistol into his belt. Orin turned back to Jeb.

"Single charge crystal?"

Jeb shook his head with a sly grin. "Double charge on that model."

Orin let out a low whistle, pulling the pistol out and weighing it in his hands. "Nice and light, even so."

Jeb nodded, sighting down the double barrel of an even larger pistol with a practiced grace. "That piece was made for you, Stone. Now, what are you thinking for the Doc?"

Everyone turned to Ari, who valiantly resisted the urge to step back only because Sally was directly behind him. He shook his head, his cheeks going cold with panic.

"Oh no. No, thank you. I am not currently in the market for an—" He lowered his voice to a whisper despite the fact that they were alone on his ship. "—illegal firearm."

Jeb threw his head back with laughter, sliding his hand into his worn leather vest to retrieve a bifold badge and holding it out for Ari's inspection.

"Relax, Doc. I'm the closest thing we got to the law around here."

Ari squinted dubiously at the badge, reading the battered inscription. "You're the local magistrate?"

Jeb closed it with a snap, tucking it back into his vest. "Sure am. Besides, these things are only illegal if you take 'em into the Core. Now I know you boys wouldn't even think of doing a thing like that, so we're all on the straight and narrow here today, Doc."

Aristotle had never spent so much time around people who seemed so averse to using his name. He found that he rather enjoyed the shocking familiarity it implied. It felt much like he had always imagined friendship might feel, if he had ever been able to make friends beyond his brother.

Orin's voice brought his focus back to the crate.

"I'm thinking something small, no kickback, definitely nonlethal."

Jeb nodded thoughtfully before selecting a miniaturized laser pistol that could fit on Ari's palm, holding it out to Ari by the snub-nosed barrel.

"Might be best to start with a garter pistol, single charge crystal, stun only."

Ari curled his fingers around it tentatively, finding the small weapon to be a surprisingly comfortable fit in his hand. "If I keep this in my garter, how will I retrieve it in the event of danger?"

Orin fumbled the surge launcher he'd been considering, and Jeb rushed to catch it with a muttered curse before carefully replacing it in the crate with a dark glare at Orin.

Orin whipped around to gape at Ari, hair falling in his face. "You"—a slow smile curled over his lips as his voice dropped low—"wearing garters, Red?"—and settled somewhere in Ari's gut. Ari blushed violently, staring down at the pistol.

"Well. Yes, I. Of course, I have the appropriate. This really isn't. I ought not discuss such things in mixed company."

He could have sworn that a tea kettle had come to a boil behind him, but it was only Sally squealing.

She bustled around Ari to sock Jeb in the arm. "I told you they were! Now, pay up!"

Jeb clucked his tongue as he locked up the crate after securing his remaining weaponry.

"Naw, see, Stone didn't know that little tidbit, which, if anything, proves they aren't. You pay up."

Sally drew her hand back for what was sure to be another sock on the arm when she was interrupted by Orin wrapping his arms around her to lift her from the ground in a massive bear hug. She patted him on the face as he set her back down on her feet, and he snagged her hand to plant a noisy kiss on her knuckles.

"Thanks for everything, Sal. I sure do appreciate all you done for us."

He picked up the crate, muscles straining in a way that even Ari could not ignore, and carried it out to the wagon below, the rest of them following in a ramshackle parade.

Dusting off his hands, Orin held one out to Jeb for a firm shake, both men nodding in synchronization.

Jeb offered Ari his hand next. "You be careful out there, Doc. Keep this one in line."

Ari quietly agreed, jumping as a small pair of arms wrapped around him tightly. Sally pulled back to pinch both sides of his cheeks, just this side of painfully.

"I could just eat you up with a spoon, hon; you're that cute!"

Ari stepped back as soon as he was released, offering a courtly bow.

"I am delighted to have made your acquaintance, Miss Mudd. Thank you for your assistance."

Sally slapped Jeb on the chest with another squeal. As Orin turned with a wave and wandered up the ramp, Sally pointed at his back, then at Ari, then at her own stony face before hopping on the wagon with a cheery wave.

Ari hurried into the ship's cabin. He picked up his garter pistol, turning it to examine the pearl handle as the ramp retracted and the bay doors closed.

Orin stepped out of the cockpit to snatch the weapon from Ari's hands and held it over his head as though Ari might make a grab for it. As if Dr. Aristotle Campbell would ever do something so ridiculously immature, especially when it was clear he could not succeed.

Orin tucked the weapon into his trouser pocket with raised brows. "Not letting you get ahold of this 'til we got time for lessons."

Ari nodded warily as Orin's small smile spread into a dimple-flashing grin, the pilot leaning one broad shoulder against the open doorway while raking over Ari's new outfit.

Orin brushed his thumb over his bottom lip, eyes flashing at Ari through thick lashes. "I'd keep this in my garter, but I really think it'd be prettier on you, don't you sweetheart?"

He turned and disappeared into the cockpit before Ari could think of a reply.

Chapter Eight

Orin twisted away from the controls as Ari settled into the copilot's chair.

"You seen Sally's list?" the pilot asked.

Ari watched as Orin pulled it up on the view screen and flicked it over to Ari's side.

Orin's side of the screen was occupied by rapidly changing numbers and complicated navigational equations as the pilot's fingers flew over the projections. He worked faster than Ari could follow.

Ari narrowed his eyes curiously. "Are you performing those calculations in your head?"

Fingers never pausing, Orin shrugged one shoulder. "Sure. Gotta recalculate our flight plan so we can make a perimeter sweep of the Verge, hit all these ratholes to see if we can hear the right song to lead us to your brother. It's a hell of a lot better plan than falling ass over tea kettle into the deep dark and flying blind in the hopes we might just trip over him."

Ari studied the list of names and locations. "Have these been rearranged?"

Orin nodded distractedly, biting his lip in concentration as he flung numbers in every direction. "Yup. Figured I'd line 'em up for us; easier to make one continuous loop than to double back every time we wanna try a new singer. Now I just gotta finish calculating our most efficient route, don't wanna waste fuel if we can help it. And, there she goes!"

He flung up his hands like a dramatic pianist finishing a complicated piece of music, tossing his hair back and dazzling in Ari's direction.

"Got our first stop pinned down. You ready to head out?"

Ari fastened his harness as Orin drew both pistols from his belt and pocket and secured them under the dash before fastening his own harness.

He sent a broad smirk Ari's way, hands poised over the controls.

"Hold on to those garters, we're gonna give Jeb And Sal a little show. It's high time me and Delilah really got to know each other."

Ari opened his mouth to ask the obvious question but didn't get a chance as his head was pushed against the headrest when the ship disengaged from the dock and immediately lifted at an unconventional speed, swooping over the dock in an elegant arc.

Orin let out a whoop, hands flying over the controls. "There we go, Delilah. Never say I couldn't show a girl a good time!"

Aristotle turned his head, fighting against the gravitational forces to face the beaming pilot. "Is Delilah the ship?"

Orin offered a pleased smile. "There you go, professor, using those brains!"

Ari adjusted back against the headrest, swiveling his chair to observe Orin caress the controls, the pilot's hands finally slowing down.

"What brought you to decide upon the name Delilah?"

Orin's face reflected off the view screen, twice as bright as the projections flying across. "Pretty name for a pretty lady, Red. And I always like to dance with the pretty ladies!"

With no more warning than a mischievous glance in Ari's direction, Orin slid them into a complicated rolling maneuver that seemed to achieve little more than rearranging Aristotle's stomach contents.

Righting the vessel, Orin patted the dash fondly. "See, Delilah knows all the steps! She and I are gonna tear it up out there."

Ari closed his eyes, relieved at the return to their previously smooth takeoff maneuvers, the creak of Orin's chair as he leaned back indicating they had exited atmosphere and autopilot had been engaged.

When he opened his eyes, Orin was checking the controls, surveying the dash almost reverently.

Ari cleared his throat, fiddling with his harness as he gathered his courage.

"Mr. Stone. I mean, Orin."

Orin unbuckled his harness as he turned his chair to face Ari, brows lifted inquisitively.

Ari suddenly didn't know what to do with his limbs, fingers clutching the harness as his feet shuffled against the base of his chair, clunky in the new, unfamiliar boots.

"I have been thinking," he said.

"Ain't exactly surprised to hear that," Orin responded with a chuckle.

Aristotle lowered his head. When he lifted his lashes to check, Orin was staring with a dazed expression, eyes flitting away when Ari caught him.

Ari focused on the line of dark stubble meandering down Orin's jawline, forcing words past the claw of anxiety in his throat. "After further consideration, I have come to the conclusion that perhaps I was too hasty in my previous decision regarding the depth of our association."

Now Orin gave him laser focus, broad hands shifting to grip his armrests so tightly the muscles jumped in his forearms. His quiet voice dropped straight down Ari's spine.

"You reckon?"

Ari nodded haltingly, fingers half releasing and then refastening the buckle on his harness repeatedly. Orin tracked the motion for a moment before pinning his attention back on Ari's red face. Ari sucked on his bottom lip, releasing it with a pop that seemed to center all of Orin's attention.

Ari heaved a shaky breath, searching for the audacity to continue.

"Indeed. I now believe that—provided we enter into any furthering of our acquaintance with the understanding that my mission and duty to my brother must come before all else—it would not be entirely inadvisable to continue exploring all aspects of our partnership."

Orin leaned forward, his chair creaking in protest. His hands released the armrests to rub fitfully at his knees.

"You're saying you changed your mind about taking part in a little meaningless diversion, sweetheart?"

Ari shivered at the heat in Orin's gaze.

"Yes," he gasped.

Orin's whispered "Thank the rusted stars" was nearly drowned out by the heavy thud of his knees hitting the metal floorboards and his hands scrambling at the buckles of Ari's flight harness.

The harness was quickly shoved aside, thick fingers moving on to the fastenings of Ari's trousers and the button at the waist of his drawers with confident precision. It was not entirely unlike the efficient way they worked the flight controls, Ari thought hysterically.

Before he could do more than choke at the transcendent sensation of Orin's rough hands sliding into the opening of his drawers, Ari found himself exposed to the cool air of the cockpit.

Orin's broad chest heaved, his eyes as reverent on Ari's flesh as they'd been upon the dash. He circled the base of Ari's cock in his thumb and forefinger, gently pulling it to stand away from his body as he studied Ari's face.

"This alright, beautiful?"

Already panting, Ari clawed at the armrests as he nodded frantically. "Yes. I. Yes, please."

Orin beamed up at him and winked before swallowing him down to the root.

Ari didn't know what to do with himself. His whole body shuddered as he was engulfed by the wet heat of Orin's mouth.

He tried to close his own mouth around the moan rising in his throat at the sight of Orin's full lips stretched around him.

Orin slid his way up to lick a wide stripe along the underside, murmuring so closely his lips dragged against the shaft. His voice dropped an octave, wrecked and filled with gravel. "Beautiful."

Ari couldn't stop shaking as Orin sucked him back down, his arms hooking under Ari's knees as large hands slid under him to shove his trousers down to his thighs and take firm hold of his ass.

Orin lifted him to his lips as though he were drinking from a cup, and Ari could only pant helplessly when he started bobbing his head. His stubble scraped against the sensitive skin of Ari's thighs, causing his heart to explore the possibility of bursting from his chest.

The waves of pleasure were building far too rapidly for Ari to do anything but be helplessly carried along.

He barely managed to stutter out, "I can't. I can't. I'm going to—" before Orin lifted honey eyes to meet his, and he was spilling down his throat, whining as Orin swallowed around him.

Orin withdrew with a little kiss to the tip, making Ari shudder once more as he collapsed back onto his folded legs on the floor.

Ari hurried to tuck himself away into his trousers as Orin eased up into the pilot's chair.

Ari chanced a glimpse at Orin to find him smiling softly, waiting until he'd caught Ari's eye before wiping his mouth on the edge of his hand with another wink and then sucking his thumb into his mouth with a contented hum.

"Knew you'd be sweet, sugar," he mumbled around it.

They both took a moment to catch their breath until Ari's gaze snagged on the prominent bulge in Orin's trousers. He slid to the edge of his chair, hesitating for a few seconds before getting clumsily to his knees between Orin's spread thighs.

Orin's lips parted in shock as he started to speak, growled instead, then cleared his throat and tried again.

"Nah, baby, you don't gotta do that. I'm alright."

Ari squared his shoulders until they pressed against the insides of Orin's thighs, lifting his chin defiantly. "What if I want to?"

Orin smoothed gentle fingers over the top of Ari's head, meeting Ari's gaze. "Well, then, I'd say please and thank you, if you would be so kind, sweetheart."

Orin was breathing so heavily the buttons were straining across his chest. He licked his lips and Ari's attention was drawn to how swollen his mouth was, a stab of desire piercing him at the sight.

Ari slid tentative hands up Orin's thighs; Orin trained on them like he was witnessing a miracle. Ari brushed his fingertips against the burning length of his cock pressed against his trousers, listening to Orin's breath hitch in his throat as the chair squeaked in protest of his iron grip on the armrests.

Orin transferred his restless hands to the outside of his thighs as Ari worked open the button fly of his trousers, peeling back the layers to expose the nest of black curls surrounding his rigid length.

Ari pulled him from his trousers, trying to stem the shaking in his hands as he discovered that his fingers could barely meet around the circumference.

The daunting size of him was not so much surprising as it was the fulfillment of Aristotle's deepest, darkest fantasies, throbbing right there in his grasp.

He wrapped both hands around, spreading his fingers until only the flushed head was exposed. He couldn't be sure whose moan was loudest at the sight.

Ari tried to get his breathing under control enough to speak, unable to tear his attention away from the bead of moisture welling from Orin's slit.

"I have a confession. I am not terribly. I have never. I haven't done this before. Or. Or anything close to this, ever."

Orin's thighs flexed against Ari's shoulders, his cock rocking forward just slightly in Ari's grasp. His voice rumbled through Ari's bones.

"You're doing great, gorgeous."

Ari peeked up through his lashes, warring between exuberance and hesitancy, and Orin zeroed in on him like a man held at gunpoint.

Ari struggled to hold his wide gaze.

"Perhaps, you could provide some guidance in the—" His gaze dropped heavily to the rosy skin inches before him, tongue tracing his lips nervously.

"—matter."

Orin sighed, one hand brushing his thick brown hair into disarray as his broad shoulders lifted into an uneven shrug.

"Listen, honey. I ain't a decent man. I really oughta be trying to talk you out of this. I'm sure if I gave you instructions, you would follow them to the letter like a damn pro, but to tell the truth, I'm just dying to watch you put that big brain to work figuring this out your own sweet self."

Ari spent a moment just looking into Orin's eyes, the hopeful, sheepish expression on his face sending warmth spreading through Aristotle's chest like an overturned inkwell.

He focused back down to the task at hand, taking a fortifying breath before leaning in to start in earnest.

He began small, with tentative kitten licks all across the head, squeezing his fingers with a deep moan as the musky scent and flavor of Orin exploded across his senses.

Orin responded with a choked gasp, his fingers compulsively clenching and releasing against his thighs.

Ari switched to one hand, moving it up and down as he licked every inch of exposed skin, his hand and chin growing sloppy wet.

He wrapped his other hand around Orin's wrist, lifting his hand to rest on the back of Ari's head. Orin groaned through his teeth, biting back other noises under the slick sound of Ari's fist working his shaft.

He cried out sharply as Ari wrapped his lips around the tip and sucked down until the head popped into his mouth.

Ari pressed down further, barely taking in a third of his length and groaning at the way his jaw already felt stretched to capacity.

Orin's bitten-back noises exploded into words, shoved rough and sweet between panting moans.

"Gorgeous. Look at you. So beautiful, baby. Holy fuck. Stars. Just, look at you."

Ari hollowed his cheeks, pressing until Orin hit the back of his throat, and when he choked, Orin's hand pulled him gently up.

Orin seemed transfixed by Ari's wet, open mouth as he shook his head. "Don't hurt yourself, baby."

Ari spared him an irritated glare before shoving himself down as far as he could go, swallowing against the choking sensation, already addicted to the blunt press of Orin against his soft palate.

Orin's fingers spasmed behind his head, Ari's eyes rolling up at the light tug to his hair. "Good. So good. You're so good for me, beautiful."

Ari attempted to bob his head as Orin had done, choking twice more before he found a rhythm that he could manage, belatedly remembering to chase the motion with his hand around the shaft.

The muscles of Orin's thighs tensed against his shoulders, the hand that wasn't on Ari's head sneaking down to slip under Ari's shirt, unerringly finding and pulling at his nipples.

Ari muffled a surprised moan at the sensation, shocked that he was hard in his trousers once again.

"Perfect, baby. Just like that."

Ari whimpered helplessly at the words, doubling his efforts.

He would feel the ache in his jaw in the morning, and the knowledge sent a dark thrill down his spine. He wanted to stay here forever, achingly full and cradled by Orin's heavy thighs.

Ari shoved his free hand under Orin's shirttails and raked his fingers through the curls up to his navel, tracing the ridges of tensing muscle across his abdomen.

Orin's voice cracked, his hand trembling against the back of Ari's head.

"Shit. Baby, you gotta pull off if you don't want. I can't. I'm close."

Ari wrapped his tongue around the head and pressed down as far as he could, hand working frantically as Orin swelled impossibly larger before shooting down his throat.

He tried to swallow against the warm waves but had to pull off to take a breath, catching the last pulse on his chin.

He lifted his lashes to fix on Orin's wild, awestruck face.

"C'mere, beautiful."

Large hands pulled Ari into his lap, evidently unconcerned with tucking himself into his trousers.

Orin grazed his sore lips with a rough fingertip before swiping at the mess on his chin.

Ari surged forward, taking Orin's tongue into his mouth as his fingers clenched in the soft waves of his hair.

Orin's hands slid into the back of his trousers before working their way to the front, blanking Ari's mind with bliss.

For the first time in his life, Aristotle couldn't hold another thought in his head until morning.

Chapter Nine

Orin woke up to the familiar sensation of a warm body in his bed, pressed close against his side.

A thoroughly ruffled crop of bright hair tickled the bottom of his chin as Ari's head shifted with every breath.

Careful not to wake him, Orin ran his fingers gently down the elegant lines of Ari's back.

Gorgeous.

His skin felt like silk, running smooth and unblemished under Orin's hands. Felt like something he ought not to be touching, to tell the truth.

Felt like something he might break with his big, clumsy hands.

Felt like something too good for the likes of him.

No denying that.

Dr. Aristotle Campbell was definitely too good for him.

Lucky for them both that Orin wasn't one to look a gift horse in the mouth. Pretty little Core scientist wants to slum it up in Orin's bed, and he wasn't going to be the one to kick him out. Man like that should come to his senses soon enough. Best not to get attached, just hold on and enjoy the ride while he could.

Damn, but he was sweet though.

Too bad he didn't come with the ship at the end of their contract.

Orin swallowed that line of thought down quicker than a shot of whiskey. No point even going there, nothing at the end of that track.

Truth was, Orin had landed himself in a real sweet spot, and he'd be a fool to throw a wrench in it by trying to make this more than it was.

Just a week ago, Orin had been cut adrift and sinking fast, no ship, no pay, no prospects.

Then he picked up on a rumor some Core stiff was hunting for a pilot with the skill and discretion to get him through the deep dark, and here he was.

Sitting pretty with a redhead in his lap and a ship coming his way when his contract was up.

Couldn't ask for better. Already getting better than he deserved, and that was a fact.

Ari lifted his head, blinking blearily up at him before busting out in a full-body flush.

Orin had never seen anything more precious.

Sweet thing was trying to keep the sheet wrapped around himself while he used his foot on the floor to scoot his trousers close enough to reach.

Orin grazed his hand along Ari's arm, ending up tangling their fingers.

"Hold up, now, beautiful, where's the fire?"

Poor thing couldn't meet his eye, slender fingers twitching before tentatively wrapping around Orin's hand. Orin's heart jumped in his chest at the gesture, dumb beast that it was.

Ari peered up at him through those spun-gold lashes as if he didn't even know the havoc that kind of thing could wreak in a man. As if he didn't even know the kind of damage he could do with a pair of pretty green eyes. As if he didn't know Orin was already doing his best not to drown in them.

Ari's morning voice was soft and sweet with just a hint of raspiness.

"Perhaps... Perhaps it would be best if I were to return to my bunk, to allow you to prepare for the day without. Without my intrusion."

Orin's chest gave a painful squeeze, sending him scrambling for something to keep Ari by his side just a little while longer. He arranged his face into a gentle smirk, brushing the hair out of Ari's face, each strand like satin beneath his fingers.

"Ain't you gonna tell me good morning, gorgeous? It's only polite."

Ari offered a tiny smile, evidently unable to decide between staring up at Orin's face and down at his bare chest.

"Good morning," he whispered.

Orin pulled on their entangled hands, drawing him closer.

Because here was the thing about Orin Stone.

He might not know much, but if there was one thing he knew, it was that good things like this didn't come by real often, and when they did, they went by real fast.

Best to keep hold of a good thing until either your grubby fingers broke or it slipped away again the way all good things did.

He brushed a kiss across Ari's forehead, keeping their fingers wrapped up in each other.

"Morning, sweetheart. C'mere."

He lifted Ari's lean body with ease, laying him on top so that every inch of their skin was touching from neck to knees.

The bright pink of Ari's skin clashed gloriously with his hair, his lips flushed a few shades darker. Orin couldn't have turned away if you paid him.

Ari ducked his head, probably to escape Orin's dumbstruck stare.

Damn. He really needed to play it cool. He'd been tripping over himself from the moment he fell into those pretty eyes, and he needed to pull up on the reins before Ari got spooked.

He needed to back off. In a minute. After Ari stopped pressing tiny little kisses under his jaw and rubbing his perfect body all over Orin like the sweetest little kitten you ever saw.

Aw, hell. He wasn't made of stone, just named for it. It'd take a better man than him to pull away now.

He could feel Ari's cock hardening against his stomach, thankful he'd gotten a good glimpse of it last night. Just as pink and pretty as the rest of him, and as sensitive as he'd ever come across.

Made him want to keep the professor in his bed for days and days, just bringing him over the edge until he turned his amazing brain to mush, all that fancy book learning set aside for a little while. Until he could only think of Orin.

They both hissed as Ari shifted, rubbing their cocks together accidentally.

Now, there was an idea.

They'd spent all night taking turns with mouths and hands, Orin's standard getting-to-know-you routine. But nothing like this. Orin could definitely get behind some full-body mutual writhing.

He took hold of Ari's hips, lifting and angling him so their cocks slotted together, the tip of Ari's nudging under Orin's cockhead with every nudge forward.

Ari pushed up to straddle him, hands braced against his chest and slender thighs forced apart by the bulk of

Orin's body, the sheets falling forgotten around Orin's knees.

Orin's mouth opened before his brain could catch up. "Yeah. That's it, baby. There you go."

Orin lifted his palm to Ari's face, gently holding it against his mouth until he caught on and started licking. Holy shit, he was pretty as a picture, pink tongue slipping out to peek between Orin's fingers, golden lashes trembling.

If he wasn't careful, his big dumb mouth would run away with him again, babbling every nonsense thought in his head. Mostly just a running commentary on how unbelievably beautiful Ari was, as if a man like that didn't already know. He was probably sick of hearing it, but Orin couldn't help himself.

He licked his palm as well for good measure before wrapping his hand around them both, pressing them tightly together.

Ari shivered, staring down at Orin's hand. Orin had been relieved to discover that, rather than being discouraged by Orin's size, he seemed to revel in it. Orin had sometimes started up with partners with a lot more experience only to have them back out when they saw what he was packing.

The corner of his mouth kicked up with pride. It'd take more than what Orin had to frighten off Dr. Aristotle Campbell.

Orin wrapped his other hand around one narrow hip, encouraging Ari to resume his rocking motion, moving his hips in tandem so they pushed together and pulled away at just the right rhythm.

The helpless little moans panting out of Ari's mouth dropped Orin's own mouth open, words pouring out like a broken dam.

"Beautiful like this. Doing so good, baby. So perfect for me."

The way Ari's eyes rolled back whenever Orin called him perfect made Orin want to do nothing but whisper it into the delicate shell of his ear for the rest of his life. Wouldn't exactly be a hardship, telling the truth all day.

Too bad he couldn't get attached.

Ari, lips parted, raked his fingers through the hair on Orin's chest before picking up the pace, watching Orin's fist avidly.

Orin matched their rhythm with his hand, pleased when Ari clutched at Orin's arm, squeezing along with the flex of his muscles, blissed-out little face like he was in heaven.

Orin could do better than that.

He rubbed his finger up under Ari's ridge, causing him to shudder and whine and fall into a million beautiful pieces, spilling onto Orin's stomach.

Orin swiped his palm through the mess before he flipped them over, hovering on his knees as he used the slick to strip his cock, rough with himself in his rush. Ari lay splayed out under him, hands gently curled and tucked up sweet on the pillow by his head. He caught Orin's eyes with a flash of green under heavy lids, lips wet and quivering with every shaky breath. Orin fell over the edge like a man riding off a cliff.

Ari barely waited for Orin to clean him off with a corner of the sheet before he was pulling his trousers on, tugging his shirt over his head with his back turned, like Orin hadn't been the one to leave that kiss stain on his hip. His skin marked up prettier than parchment, and Orin couldn't wait to leave his signature.

Ari turned with his boots dangling from one hand, the rest of his clothing bundled under his arm. He attempted to smooth his hair as he took a deep breath, Orin grinning at the way it sprang back up defiantly.

"I should. Thank you for. For an exceptionally pleasant interlude. I really should get back to my lab now, stop wasting so much time," he said haltingly, unable to decide between examining the floor or Orin's face.

Orin pushed at the hurt that bubbled up at being considered a waste of time. No sense expecting anything more. Not much different than being a meaningless diversion, tell the truth.

He held out his hand, black silk ribbon garter dangling from his fingers.

"Ain't you forgetting something, sweetheart?"

Ari snatched it with a return of his fiery blush, casting one more shy glance over his shoulder as he rushed from the room.

Orin fell back on the bed with a sigh, beating down the rising tide of feelings that wouldn't do any good to anybody, resigning himself to spending the rest of the day reviewing his flight calculations for errors.

*

He had been doing just that for hours, hunched over his pad at the little table in the main cabin and stuffing his face, when he was interrupted by a shout from the end of the corridor.

Aristotle burst out of his laboratory like a man possessed, hair sticking up around the brass safety goggles shoved on top of his head.

His shaking hands clutched a roll of parchment which he struggled to spread open as he hurried over to throw himself into the seat across from Orin with no regard for the effect his flailing limbs might have on Orin's lunch.

"I've got it. I have. I really have, this time. I-I-I-I found him! Look at this. Look!"

Orin cautiously lowered his gaze to the parchment, suppressing a wince at the loopy Core script scrawled haphazardly across. The notes had been written by an increasingly unsteady hand, the lines getting shakier toward the bottom of the parchment.

Ari watched him expectantly, the whites of his eyes visible all the way around. He leaned in excitedly.

"You see? The data from the samples gives away his location!"

Orin nodded slowly, trying to subtly push the parchment away from himself and closer to Ari.

"Yeah. Yup, I see that. Sure do. But, just for the sake of clarity, why don't you break it down for me?"

Ari nodded like his head was on a spring, goggles sliding off the back of his head to land on the floor with a concerning crunch as he pushed to stand.

"Yes. Yes, of course. I'll just fetch my pad, shall I?"

The question appeared to be rhetorical as he was already careening back down the hallway to the lab, returning in moments with only the sound of something falling with the echo of breaking glass left behind.

This time, he slid onto the bench beside Orin, the force of his enthusiasm alone enough to shift Orin's bulk all the way to the edge.

His long, pale fingers trembled as he activated the pad, pulling up layers of projections, some of which, Orin was relieved to see, were written in standard block.

The pad rattled against the table as Ari balanced it against the edge with one hand, his entire body practically vibrating.

"As you can see here, I was able to retrieve samples *A*, *B*, and *C* from the site of the abduction. Sample *B* turned out to have been soil from Britannia, but I had been unable to properly identify samples *A* and *C*. Until today!"

Orin nodded, trying to fold himself smaller to make room for Ari on the bench.

"I was able to identify sample *C* after our initial foray onto the Verge, standard sediment from simulated iron ore, found on most man-made settlement structures on the Verge. But this"—Ari's fingers flung projections left and right as he zoomed in on a baffling chemical formula—"sample *A*. It's the key. Because I knew. I knew he had gone beyond the Verge. But where? That was the question. Sample *A* is the answer. Tantalum."

Orin blinked. Ari took this as encouragement.

"Tantalum! Illegal in the Core, illegal to transport across the Verge. Because where does it originate?"

Understanding crept along the back of Orin's mind like a thief in the night, bludgeon lifted to knock him off his ass.

Ari's eyes grew wilder and wilder, green glowing with an unholy light as he continued.

"The Restricted Sector! Of course!"

Orin turned as much as he could in the limited space of the bench, resting his arm over the top, fingertips brushing against Ari's vibrating shoulders.

He gave a disbelieving frown. "You think your brother was taken to the Restricted Sector?"

It would be generous to say Ari nodded when, really, he did his level best to fling his head from his neck by sheer force of enthusiasm.

"Yes! You see, the reason I could not properly identify sample *A* was because in my initial haste I had falsely identified it as niobium! I'm not a chemist, you understand; I'm a geologist. I merely minored in chemistry in my undergraduate studies. That's why it took me so long to determine the minute but crucial differences. Niobium tells me nothing. Tantalum tells me everything!"

Orin tightened his lips against the sinking sensation in his gut. The hope on his little face was so bright, he had to squint against it. Damn, but he didn't want to be the man to shut that hope down. He tried to speak clearly and quietly.

"I'm real glad you found a clue, sweetheart, but even if you know where he went, you still need to find the right exit point. We gotta listen for a song to lead the way out. Can't just jump the Verge blind and hope we hit the jackpot."

Ari gripped Orin's arm, surprising strength in his delicate hands.

"So that's what we do. We follow your loop to find the exit point, gather some more information to pinpoint his location. Then we jump the Verge and follow your navigational calculations into the Restricted Sector. This is why I engaged your services—to navigate past the Verge. You said you knew your way around the deep dark; now I just need you to get us through to the other side."

Orin pulled his arm away, worrying the corner of his lip with his thumb as he frowned, a nervous habit he usually tried to keep better control of. Aristotle Campbell was proving to have a distinctly negative impact on Orin's control.

"No, see, this is not what we agreed on. This isn't some little trip past the Verge. This ain't just dipping our toes in the deep dark and skipping back home. You're talking about breaking into the Restricted Sector. Real restricted. The kinda restricted that means we'd be banned from the Core and sent away to rot in a Verge prison for the rest of our days. If we're lucky."

Ari shrugged, acting more like they were discussing what to have for supper than contemplating the possibility of making life-ruining decisions. "That's only if we are caught."

Orin couldn't help his eyes going round as rivets.

"If we're caught? Are you listening to yourself? Holy shit, Red. You'd think since I've gotten real close and personal with the area that I would've noticed those ten-pound balls you've been lugging around."

Ari leveled him with a look Orin could've sworn he'd been too innocent to give just the day before, taking a tour of Orin's body before landing back on his face with a lifted brow.

"Perhaps you simply haven't been paying attention."

Chapter Ten

Ari checked and rechecked his findings. There was no longer any doubt. Theo had been taken to the Restricted Sector. Theo's sparse and hurried notes indicated he'd been abducted by an Outlier, but Ari had still held out hope that he'd misinterpreted the description.

He pulled up Theo's clumsily scrawled notes on his pad.

Tattoos, bizarre clothing, Restricted tech, and now, traces of tantalum. Theo had not been mistaken. Some might have been preoccupied at this point by attempting to determine why an Outlier would have any interest in a linguist from Britannia, but Ari couldn't begin to care.

The only important thing was for him to find his brother, safe and sound. The rumors and mystery surrounding the Restricted Sector and the Outliers who dwelled within did not inspire confidence in Theo's safety. Whispers carried across the Verge and throughout the Core of slavery and forced augmentation, dangerous tech and moral corruption. Ari could only hope such rumors were just that and nothing more.

He was relieved that the confirmation of Theo's destination did not increase his panic but helped him to focus. Ari had a goal now. A fixed target. He just needed to make his way there.

Orin had been understandably resistant to the change of plans. The only thing Aristotle could do was to alter their agreement. He had been prepared to get on his knees and beg or employ other newfound skills when Orin had reluctantly relented and agreed upon their new verbal contract.

Ari was no longer quite as disgusted by the exchange of bodily fluids to seal the deal.

Orin agreed to get Ari across the deep dark and into the Restricted Sector, but that was where they would part ways. Ari would have to arrange his own way home after he located Theo. The ship, or rather, Delilah, would belong to Mr. Stone from the moment Ari disembarked inside the Sector.

It was a fair trade, as far as Ari was concerned. He was asking Orin to take an enormous risk. The threat of Enforcers alone was enough of a deterrent before considering the unknown dangers of the deep dark and the Restricted Sector. It was the least Ari could do to let him have the ship and be done with Aristotle and his problems as soon as possible.

Ari stomped down firmly on the trickle of dread that crept through his chest at the notion of Orin leaving. It was settled. There was no point in wallowing over something that hadn't happened yet. Ari could take the time to fall apart once Theo was back home and no sooner.

He had to be practical, treat the physical aspect of their partnership as casually as Orin did. Ari nodded to himself as he carefully packed up his lab equipment. That was exactly what he would do. Simple.

He just needed to refrain from allowing his emotions to become engaged.

He left the lab, closing the door behind him before heading into the cockpit. Orin was already seated in the pilot's chair, hunched over a new set of calculations with numbers and equations flying across the screen. He offered up a smile when Ari entered, his flashing dimples having no effect on Ari's heart.

The fluttering in his chest was likely due to indigestion from too many dehydrated foods. Ari's emotions remained entirely disengaged. According to plan.

Ari took his seat, watching Orin's hands move across the screen for just a moment longer than was strictly necessary. He had decided to keep his emotions from becoming engaged, not his vision.

Or any of his senses really.

Ari swallowed awkwardly, pulling up their revised list for consideration. "Do we have an initial destination in mind? To locate a singer?"

Orin didn't turn his head, but amusement crinkled up the skin at the corner of his eye in a way Ari should not have found as attractive as he did.

"Yup. Sure do. Got a couple places lined up all in a row for us. I'm just finishing up on these practice navigations, keeping myself sharp before we have to hit the deep dark."

Ari squinted at the impossible-to-interpret numbers and symbols. "All of this is just practice?"

Orin nodded. "Yeah. Something I used to do for fun, keep myself from getting bored. Calculate how to get from here to there, imaginary ships and imaginary places. Get your numbers right, and you can go anywhere you please. Get your calculations right, and you can always get away."

His voice trailed off as a wash of color rose up the back of his neck, hands swiftly closing down his projections as he kept his face turned away from Ari.

"Sorry 'bout that. Catch me jabbering away on this nonsense. I know how you hate to waste your time. Let's get started on finding that singer."

Ari pursed his lips. There was something there, in Orin's words that niggled at him. Something defensive in his voice, as though he expected Ari to reprimand him. It made something twist unpleasantly in Ari's gut.

He turned his attention to the projection Orin had brought up on the main view screen.

"This here's a good place to start. Big settlement, lots of people, lots of hiding places, lots of songs on the wind. Figured we could hit up two or three ratholes first thing in the morning. I've got us headed there now. If I can time it right, and I always do, sugar, we oughta make landfall just before dawn."

Ari nodded his head, the settlement was one of the few on the Verge he'd heard of, infamous for its colorful clash of cultures and seething pool of illegal activities.

Orin indicated Ari's screen with his chin. "Need to get ourselves a list of songs we're listening for. What do we have to go on?"

Ari opened up Theo's notepad. "We need any information we can find on Outliers and exit points, anything related to the Restricted Sector. My brother left something of a description of his abductor, as well as some odd sketches. I would like to see if anyone knows anything about these images."

Orin swiveled his chair and leaned forward, elbows balanced on spread knees. "He left a description? You got a note from him?"

Ari flicked over to Theo's note, hesitating before enhancing the image. Orin skimmed over the words before honing in on the images.

"Huh. Never seen nothing quite like that before."

Ari nodded, moving in closer to study the images. "Precisely why I am hoping someone might be able to offer more information."

Orin rubbed his chin thoughtfully, sitting up in his chair. "Alright, so we ask around about this Outlier fella, flash those drawings at the right singer. What about your brother? You got some pics or vid for us to show? Might help if you give me a description too."

Ari closed the notes and powered down his screen before turning his head to answer.

"No description should be necessary, as Theo and I are identical twins. I shall simply refer to myself as a visual aid in jogging their memories."

Ari paused as Orin's face did something decidedly odd.

"Twins?" he gasped out quietly. Orin gaped like he had been struck on the back of the head, mouth wide open and slack with shock. "You're telling me there's two of you?"

Aristotle shook his head sharply, reclining back in his seat to cross his arms over his narrow chest. "Of course not, don't be ridiculous. We are two distinct people, different in many ways."

Orin shut his mouth, the prominent lump of his Adam's apple bobbing in his throat. His hands gestured clumsily in Ari's direction.

"Yeah, no, I get that, honey, but you're saying he looks just like you. Like if the two of you were to stand side by side in front of me, I'd be seeing double."

Ari shrugged irritably. "I suppose. We are identical, but Theo has always worn his hair longer. You would be able to tell us apart, I'm sure. Our close resemblance should be sufficient for anyone who may have seen Theo, however."

Orin nodded distractedly, busy admiring Ari's face and figure.

Ari shoved past the pilot more roughly than was necessary as he stalked out of the cockpit. "Please wipe that stupid expression from your face. The concept of twins can hardly be a revelation to you."

As he followed slowly, the thump of Orin's boots echoed heavily after Ari's more precise footsteps. "I'm just savoring the knowledge that not only have I met the prettiest man in existence, but that apparently somewhere out there is another one just as pretty. I'm waking up tomorrow to a more beautiful world, and that's a fact."

Ari walked into the galley and opened a cabinet, realized he didn't want anything, and slammed it shut again. "Yes, well, if you manage to do your job properly, you will get to meet him as soon as possible."

Humming in acknowledgement, Orin settled onto the bench, knees spread wide as he faced Ari.

Ari caught his wide smirk and sighed. "What?"

Orin's grin popped his dimples in full display. "I'm just sitting here contemplating the possibility that I could be the cream filling in a you sandwich."

Ari swiveled indignantly to stare agape at his companion. "You are disgusting!"

Reclining in his seat, Orin slid his pelvis to tilt in Ari's direction at the edge of the bench, a deep sound of approval rumbling in his chest.

"Love it when you talk dirty to me, baby."

Ari pushed away from the cabinet, face burning as he sped down the corridor to scramble for his door panel. He rushed through the narrow opening before the door had finished sliding open.

Ari stood in the middle of his room with clenched fists, occasionally scrubbing against the tears running down his face. He didn't know how long he stood in such idleness before stumbling into his en suite.

Water trickled slowly into the tiny basin; Ari cut the flow after a few ounces had collected. Water was precious this close to the Verge.

He bent in half over the sink to rinse his swollen eyes, cupping the cool water in his palm and blinking into it, lashes brushing the skin at the base of his thumb.

He had begun to repeat the procedure on the other side when he heard a knock at his door.

Leaving the water in the basin, Ari walked the short distance to his door panel and stared at the controls until another knock sounded, fainter than the first.

He sighed and slapped the panel, then turned away to wipe his face against the sleeve of his shirt as the door slid open.

Big boots clunked into his berth as the door hissed closed again.

When Ari turned, Orin was standing as far away as the limited space allowed, head still ducked from entering the room.

He had tucked his hands away in his front trouser pockets, broad shoulders folded in toward his chest.

Ari held his wrists behind his back as he lifted his chin to wait.

He didn't wait long.

"Shit, I'm sorry, Red."

Aristotle sniffed disdainfully. "I'd prefer to receive your apology without expletives."

Orin's mouth formed around another filthy word of frequent use before swallowing it back. He compressed his full lips into a thin line before speaking again.

"I'm sorry."

Aristotle nodded and moved to sit on the edge of his narrow bunk. He plucked at a loose thread in his sleeve.

"I know you didn't mean anything by it, truly. It's simply that, he's my brother, and I miss him dearly. I won't hear an unkind word about him, not from you or anyone else."

Orin approached, his bulk filling the meager space of Ari's chambers.

"Wasn't meant to be unkind, but I know it wasn't respectful. I won't talk like that about him again, alright?"

Ari nodded, then leaned into the rough palm that lifted against his cheek.

"You been crying, beautiful?"

Rather than reply, Ari turned to brush his lips against the thick pad of Orin's thumb.

Orin bent down, eyes on Ari's lips, but Ari jerked away, pressure rising in his chest.

"I'm sorry. I shouldn't have implied that I was seeking physical intimacy. I'm afraid I'm not going to be good company right now, and—"

Orin's finger was gentle against his lips, the careful tenderness contrasting beautifully with the roughness of his skin.

"Hush now. It's alright. We don't gotta do that right now."

Ari shook his head, and Orin stepped closer, tucked Ari's face into his shoulder with a wide palm over the base of his skull.

Ari stiffened, but Orin just shifted until he was held more securely in his arms, face pressed against the warm, worn linen of his shirt.

He raised his hands to Orin's back, clutching the fabric over his shoulder blades tightly.

The first sob took Ari by surprise, both of them freezing as it seemed to echo across the metal panels of his bunk.

The second and third began a tidal wave that pulled Ari under helplessly, quickly soaking the fabric over Orin's shoulder as he shook violently in his arms.

Orin only stepped closer, wrapping Ari so tightly his heels left the floor, making soft shushing noises as he pressed his cheek to the top of Ari's head.

Ari had never felt so simultaneously terrified and utterly safe.

The terror had been a constant from the moment he'd discovered his brother had disappeared.

It was the sensation of safety that he feared could prove the most dangerous.

Chapter Eleven

Ari stretched across the bed, tensing as his fingers met nothing more than cold sheets. He cast about the room for any sign of Orin but it was as though he had never been there, everything neatly in its place. Ari's clothing had been carefully folded and stacked next to his boots near the door.

He blushed to think of Orin folding his underthings and then blushed harder when he considered exactly why that was the height of foolishness.

A muffled thud and clanking sounds came through the door, and Ari hurried to get dressed enough to investigate. He poked his head through the door to squint into the corridor in his shirtsleeves and trousers, stocking feet peeking out beneath.

The muted sounds were coming from his lab.

Ari slapped the entry panel and peered warily through the door to find his pilot had pried open a random selection of the cabinet panels built into the wall, rummaging inelegantly through his lab supplies.

Ari's hackles rose as he drew himself to his full height before rushing to halt the desecration of his inner sanctum.

"Just what do you think you are doing?" he demanded in a tone that was completely authoritative and not at all shrill.

Orin tossed an unconcerned smile over his shoulder, holding meticulously labeled parcels of laboratory equipment in each enormous fist.

"You keep your med supplies in here, right, professor?"

Ari nodded, mouth working around words that refused to manifest beyond an indignant squeak as Orin shoved the parcels back into the cabinet before yanking open the next panel.

Ari shoved past his broad shoulders and plastered himself with arms spread wide against the once sacred wall of lab storage.

"Stop this at once!"

Orin cocked one eyebrow at him before reaching nonchalantly over Ari's head to pop open another storage panel and pick through the contents with absolutely no concern for Aristotle's organizational systems.

Ari reached up and wrapped his fingers around one thick wrist, ignoring the odd tingle in his stomach as both of his hands were required to complete the circumference. He looked up at Orin, eyelids fluttering with dismay.

"Please."

Orin's mouth slid open, staring down at Ari as he hung stubbornly from his wrist. An unexpected wash of color spread across the crest of his stubbled cheeks before he lowered his arm and took a step back, clearing his throat.

"I'm just searching for your jabs, assumed you'd have the deluxe set somewhere on board. You seem the type to be overprepared."

Ari released his grip at the roll of muscle beneath his fingertips, glancing down to watch Orin clench and release his hand restlessly against his thigh. Ari then turned to begin setting things to rights, resigning himself to reserving time in his lab schedule for a complete reorganization. He gestured to the panel closest to the doorway on their right.

"The med kit and any other medical supplies are stored in there. I suppose I should have informed you of their whereabouts in case of emergency."

He whirled in place at a sudden thought. "Are you injured again? Do you need my assistance?"

Orin had already turned his back to continue rummaging through the med supply panel. He shook his head distractedly. "Nah. I'm right as rain, myself. Just on the hunt for—ah!—these."

He displayed the deluxe hypodermic injection kit Ari had purchased at the ship supply when he and Theo had first begun outfitting the ship for exploration.

Ari pushed his lips to the side in confusion. "Why do you need emergency jabs? You're not up to date on yours? We could visit a physician when we make landfall."

Orin shook his head, wrestling the package open. "Don't you worry about me, sugar. I'm all up to date. Fit as a damned fiddle." He inspected each syringe before dropping them into a soft leather bag attached to his hip.

He then held up four matching syringes with a triumphant grin, each one standing proudly from between his fingers as though displaying a clever card trick.

"Now these are what we'll be needing, where we're going."

Ari squinted at the jabs, shock running through him at the label. "Those are for the prevention of sexually transmitted diseases."

Orin dropped them in his bag and pointed both index fingers at Ari. "Bingo, professor!"

He turned and walked down the corridor, his off-tune whistling ringing against the metal panels.

Ari hurriedly shut the med supply cabinet panel and followed on his heels.

"Why do you think we would need... Wait, where are we going?"

*

The settlement was as different from Sally's little town as it was from Britannia. Same artificial atmo sky and manufactured rust dirt roads, but there the resemblance ended.

The streets teemed with life, scores of people hurrying by or loudly haggling at the rust-dappled market stands crammed right on top of one another in the narrow space between buildings.

The buildings rose up to three stories high, their wooden siding and metal roofing lending an air of cohesiveness to the architecture. Large metal signs proclaimed a variety of shops and trades.

Ari squinted at a sign that was either painted with a coiled snake or a length of rope, trying to determine which it could be and what might be found inside.

"Keep up, Red! Slower than a cart with three busted wheels, I swear."

Orin's voice cut through the crowd ahead, and Ari scurried to catch up, bobbing his head at a passing lady who blew him a kiss in response, giggling and twirling her patchwork parasol.

He caught up to Orin quickly, suspecting the pilot had shortened his stride so he could do so. Ari resisted the urge to reach for his arm as though he were being escorted through the park back home.

Their arms bumped together, and Orin looked down, cocking his eyebrow and bending his elbow in Ari's direction as if he'd read his mind. Ari studied the ground and shoved his hands in his pockets. Orin seemed to hesitate before dropping his arm and picking up the pace once again.

He cut through the crowded street effortlessly despite his size, smooth as a fish through a stream. Ari envied his ease, having felt wrong-footed from the moment they stepped out onto the busy dock.

Orin hopped up the steps of one of the taller buildings which bore no sign, Ari following at a more respectable climb. The corrugated roofing over the porch had rusted through in large enough spots that hints of green sky shone through.

Orin knocked on the door sharply three times before turning back to Ari.

"Almost guaranteed to hear a good song in this house, professor."

A tightly corseted woman opened the door and scanned the pair of them suspiciously before her face lit with joy as she flung her naked arms around Orin's neck. Orin responded in kind, lifting her off the ground with a booming laugh.

Ari attempted not to stare at the fact that the woman was standing on her porch in broad daylight wearing nothing but several layers of ruffled undergarments beneath her exposed blue corset.

She was still laughing as she backed into the house, throwing her elaborately braided black hair over her shoulder. "Come on in, boys! Can't tell you how much we missed you round these parts, Orin Stone!"

Orin guided Ari inside with a firm hand against his lower back. "And I'm pleased as punch to see you, Miss Violet. Been too long. How's your sister? Last I was here, she was feeling poorly as I recall."

Miss Violet's smile emphasized the cracking ruby paint on her mahogany cheeks. Flecks of gold glitter loosened and peeled away as she spoke. "She's doing much better, thanks to you, darling."

Orin nodded, keeping his hand pressed to Ari's back. "Glad to hear it. Who's on today?"

Miss Violet's eyes cut to Ari and back up to Orin before she turned and led the way through heavily fringed crimson curtains into a large parlor. The room held an upright piano with a distinct leftward lean and various poly-brocade chaise longues. She gestured at the dozen half-naked people assembled on them.

"Got some new faces on today, like to give 'em the day shift 'til they get accustomed to the art of entertaining. You probably remember Gladys though."

She pointed at a petite girl spilling out of her corset, with hair brighter than Ari's but in a distinctly artificial hue, curled up and bored to tears on one of the lounges.

Orin's lips kicked up at the corner. "Sure do, Miss Violet. Real nice girl, Gladys. Listen, any chance you heard a singer goes by the name of Hinge?"

Miss Violet stepped back, planting one hand on the curve of her hip. "You must need a song real bad if you're willing to listen to that weasel. Jeanie's got him upstairs, you'll have to wait 'til he's done with his appointment. Be done in a half hour, man's real punctual."

Orin smirked at that, taking his hand from Ari's back to remove the leather pouch from his belt. "We sure would appreciate it if you could send him our way. I got something for you, courtesy of the professor here. I know times are hard."

He held out the bag to Miss Violet who took it with a caution, both eyes and lips widening as she looked inside.

Her gaze shot back up to Orin, glittering to better effect than the flakes on her cheeks.

"Why, you're an angel. An honest angel. My stars, but we needed these. Local sawbones cleared town near three weeks past. Some of my new faces been riding on a prayer."

Orin cupped her shoulder with one big hand, squeezing affectionately. "Next time that happens, you buzz my com. I'll get you fixed up soon as I can."

Miss Violet placed her hand over Orin's, multicolored bangles clinking musically. "I'll keep that in mind."

Orin dropped his hand to his pocket and pulled out a paper-wrapped parcel.

"Brought something for the little ones too. Just a pack of fizzy pops. How many y'all got in the house now?"

Miss Violet took the parcel gladly, tucking it down the front of her corset as Ari stared resolutely at the wall over her head.

"Got four underfoot now that Eben is gone apprenticing. All but the baby are down at the schoolhouse."

Orin's face lit brighter than the electric candles flickering along the walls. "Good, that's real good. Get all those books in their heads, give 'em all a fighting chance."

Miss Violet's answering smile had an edge to it. "I'm gonna make damn sure not one of 'em ends up working for me, darling. That's a promise."

Ari edged closer to Orin as a young man approached from across the parlor, watching Ari from beneath gold-painted lids. Ari gasped quietly as he was wearing even less than Miss Violet, his small rouged nipples peeking out over a short gold corset.

Orin glanced up, intercepting the seductive pout Ari was receiving. With a chuckle, he turned back to Miss Violet, slinging his arm around Ari's waist. The young man slinked back to his chaise with a sigh. Orin pulled Ari in close as Ari clutched at his arm.

"Got somewhere quiet we can wait it out? My partner ain't exactly used to being entertained."

Miss Violet scanned Ari from head to toe, dancing eyes catching on Orin's arm around his waist.

"Why don't you head on back to Gladys' room? She's about to take her break. I'll be sure to send the weasel up soon as I can."

Orin thanked her with a nod, arm keeping Ari close as he led them to the narrow staircase rising up through the entryway. They climbed into an even narrower hallway, passing three doors before entering one that, as far as Ari could tell, was entirely indistinguishable from the others.

Orin released his grip on Ari to close the door behind them and scanned the room before walking to a set of shelves set into the wall beside the fireplace.

Ari nervously took in their surroundings, cataloguing the draped bed and pair of chairs set beside a small table as the only furniture. A single window let in enough light that he didn't need to hit the panel to the gold-painted sconces.

Ari chewed on his lip, bursting with questions and entirely unsure whether any of them might be well received. He chose the detail that stuck out to him as most unexpected.

"How did you know there would be children here?"

Orin scratched at his elbow, busily searching the shelves in front of them.

"There's always children in a bawdy house. Byproduct of the business."

The glance he tossed over his shoulder was brittle around the edges. He continued on as he reached up to shuffle a few bottles aside on the middle shelf.

"No matter how hard folks work to prevent it. Most of the time, the little ones that make themselves useful get to stick around for a while."

Ari's blood ran cold. "Useful?"

Orin shook his head slowly, fingers wrapped around a dusty blue bottle he carefully lifted from the shelf, easing the others back into place.

"Not like that. At least, not here."

His eyes grew distant before he gave his head another small shake. He held the bottle aloft as he indicated the rickety wooden table with a jerk of his chin.

"Bawdy house kids can keep a roof over their head if they've got a talent for something like sneaking through pockets, or if they're built like a solid steel engine block like I was. Then they can work security. No grown man expects to be thrown out on his ass by a kid. Learned from a tender age how to thrive on the element of surprise."

All the other questions fell out of Ari's head as he sank into one of the spindly legged chairs.

"You were raised in a place like this?"

Orin threw his head back to take a swig from the bottle before pushing it across the table to Aristotle.

"Mmm, wouldn't say I was raised. People don't raise weeds that sprout up where they aren't wanted. Not like they'd raise a sweet little flower such as yourself."

Ari sipped from the bottle, forcing himself to swallow the burning liquid, tears welling over from the effort.

Orin swiped the bottle from his hand, muscled the stopper back down the neck, and set it on the floor beneath his chair.

"Might say I grew up in a place like this. Well, not exactly like this." He gestured at the moth-eaten draperies and heavy crimson bedclothes. "This place has boards on the floors and fripperies on the windows. This is much more of an upscale establishment than we had back home. Still, seems I grew up alright. Last I checked I was full grown, at least."

He lifted his right arm to flex and wink at Ari, who was momentarily distracted by the bulging bicep on display before a distant moan reminded him of exactly where they were sitting.

"Though it does seem to shed light on your distinctive vocabulary, I admit to some surprise that you spent your formative years in a—" His voice dropped to a scandalized whisper. "—house of pleasure."

Orin's brow grew two vertical lines, his gaze directed inward. "Wouldn't say that either. Not much pleasure to be had in a place like this, not for the folks that live here. Certainly not where I come from."

Aristotle leaned forward with keen interest. "Where exactly do you come from? I know you grew up on the Verge, but I still don't know which settlement."

Orin's chair legs scraped back across the floor, knocking the bottle over to roll with a dull *thunk* against the cold brick of the hearth. He patted his spread knees, practiced smirk firmly in place.

"Enough talk, sweetheart. Why don't you come over here, and we can make better use of our time? Wouldn't touch those sheets with a borrowed stick, but there's plenty of room for you right here."

He hooked his thumb behind the button placket of his trousers before trailing the other hand suggestively down his thigh.

Ari ignored the gesture, focused on Orin's face. The pilot appeared a study in relaxation, face pulled into a casual smirk. He was posed just as he had been when Aristotle had approached him a week before in the saloon, every inch of him entirely confident and without a care.

Ari was surprised by his ability to see the act for what it was.

Chapter Twelve

The weasel comparison was not inaccurate.

Hinge twitched his pointed nose as he gave Ari a once-over, wiping sweat from his brow. He held out his damp hand to shake, but Ari just stared in disgust, bolting from the chair to the other side of the room as Orin shook in silent amusement.

Orin slapped Hinge's outstretched palm with a hearty shake.

"Word is you might have a song for the right ear."

Hinge slinked onto the chair Ari had vacated, narrow shoulders bowed inward. He offered a gap-toothed grin, raking fingers through his greasy hair.

"Depends what you wanna hear. Depends what you're willing to pay."

His rheumy eyes slid to Ari with a smirk.

"Looks to me like your new fancyman could afford a real sweet song, Stone. Looks to me like you dug him straight outta the Core. Now, there's a song I'd like to hear; what's it like to catch a ride on a genuine Core bitch?"

Orin leaned forward so sharply and suddenly that the table screeched several inches across the floor to dig into Hinge's belly. The expression on Orin's face could have been called a smile simply from the sheer number of teeth on display, were a person to have no other concept of the word smile.

"I'll remind you to keep a civil tongue in your head, and I ain't gonna say it twice."

Hinge gave a twitchy nod, finding the surface of the table suddenly fascinating.

Orin sat back in his chair, arms crossed in such a way that put his bulging muscles on display, the sight having a vastly different impact on each of the two other occupants in the room.

Ari approached quietly. Resting his hands on the back of Orin's chair, he was bolstered by the way Orin leaned back slightly to press his shoulders against Ari's knuckles.

Orin inclined his head to indicate Ari. "You ever seen him before? Ever heard a song about him?"

Hinge considered Ari carefully, suppressing his leer after a sharp movement from Orin's boot against the table.

"'Fraid not. I'd remember hearing such a pretty song."

Orin nodded, and Ari tightened his fingers on the chair. "My partner and I are listening for a couple songs in particular. Anything on the wind about the Restricted Sector?"

Hinge flinched, cautious squint shooting to the door and back to Orin's face.

"That's the kinda singing gets your throat slit. Not sure you can afford that kinda song, Stone."

"Let's say I can," Orin said quietly.

Hinge licked his lips.

"One hundred credits."

Orin's laugh shook the table.

"Bullshit. Forty."

"Eighty, and that's better than you deserve."

Orin leaned forward, pushing the table into the soft flesh of Hinge's belly.

"Sixty, or we walk. There's a dozen better singers down the street, and you know it."

Hinge gave an ugly leer, casting over Ari up and down. "Hope he's worth it, Stone. I don't much appreciate your boot on my neck." He checked around the empty room before leaning over the table.

"Songs I been hearing lately all got the same tune— all about how the Restricted Sector been opening up. Outlier trash been pouring in like they think they can blend in with us Verge rats. Like we can't see them for the freaks they are, marked up like that."

Ari fumbled for his notes, opening his pad and pulling up Theo's drawings. "Markings like these?"

Hinge nodded, lip lifted with disgust. "Yeah, some are like that; look like they been scribbled on with ink, 'cept it's seeped in. Part of their skin like their disgusting tech."

Ari zoomed in on the images. "Can you tell us anything about these specific markings?"

Hinge leaned closer, rubbing his chin. He pointed at the design of wandering parallel lines and small circles. "Lots of 'em got that shit, some kinda circuitry under their skin. Half machine, is what they are, barely human."

Ari frantically added to his notes as Orin tapped on the table.

"Any songs telling why they're coming? Didn't used to see Outliers much at all outside the deep dark."

Hinge scratched at a dotted rash on his neck irritably. "Ain't heard nothing specific, but I can tell you this. The bastards are real scared, all of em. Running from something bad enough that crossing the Verge seems like a better option. You oughta know more than most, Stone, just how bad that's gotta be."

Orin stiffened in his chair before reaching back for Ari's pad and then holding it out to Hinge in a firm grasp.

"Ident. You'll receive seventy credits. Thanks for the song."

Hinge pressed his fingers to the pad, waiting impatiently for the beep before tearing away and scuttling out of the room like something was nipping at his heels.

Ari took his pad back with shaking hands and checked that he had added everything to his notes before closing it and tucking it away.

Orin watched him quietly for a few moments, then brought his arm up around Ari's hips to pull him into his lap. Ari melted into the embrace, winding his fingers in the opening of Orin's shirt as he pressed his face to his neck.

Orin bundled him close to his chest. "I know you were hoping to hear the perfect song on our first try, but that just ain't how it works. We gotta go listen some more before it'll all come together."

Ari nodded, mumbling against Orin's throat. "Yes, of course. Of course, you're right. I appreciate the way you took the lead in dealing with that weasel."

Orin's hand ghosted over the nape of Ari's neck. "Anything for you, Red."

Both of their heads snapped to the door at the sudden flurry of rapid knocking, Orin's hand dropping from Ari's neck to the pistol at his hip.

Ari stood to approach the door but was startled by Orin's hand firm around his wrist. He guided him to stand against the wall beside the door. Orin's pistol made a low buzzing hum as he clicked the charge with his thumb.

Orin held the barrel against his hip, pointed straight ahead as he palmed the door open. The buzzing hum switched off with a click when Gladys bustled inside, deliberately sliding her scandalously exposed bosom across Orin's front as she entered.

Orin tucked his pistol back in his belt holster and leaned against the wall cheerfully. "Kicking us out, Glad?"

Gladys twirled a curl around her finger as she took the scenic route up from Orin's boots. "Got a client in a few minutes. No time for freebies today, Stone. Much as I'd like to say otherwise." Her shining brown eyes were rimmed with black, painted lips curled sweetly.

Orin's gaze darted to Ari, shifting awkwardly in his place beside the door. "That's fine. I'm not exactly in the market right now. On a job, and all."

Now, those carefully lined eyes fixed on Ari, disarming buck teeth showing as her grin spread as wide as it could go.

"We all seen your new job, honey. Hope this one lasts a while. 'Bout time you got a nice payout, if you ask me."

Orin laughed off the comment as he guided Ari out of the house with one broad hand open across his back. He dropped his hand as soon as they hit the street, leaving a cold spot that only seemed colder for the memory of the heat of his hand.

Ari refused to dwell on how much he missed it already.

The next "rathole" on the list didn't even require them to move their ship from the dock. Orin led them down the street to a single-story building dug in between two taller businesses. One of the corrugated metal shutters, which hung over the two small windows, fell off with a bang as the door shut behind them.

"Stay here. Try to be casual," Orin said, leaving Ari to stand by the door as he sauntered over to the bar.

Ari had thought Orin's distinctive walk, led entirely by the hips, was indicative of his Verge upbringing, but he was coming to understand it was simply a characteristic of Orin himself. Ari found it distracting at the most inopportune times, struggling to peel himself away to survey the dark tavern.

He broke a sweat trying different poses in the pursuit of being casual while Orin appeared to get into an argument with the barkeep. Ari jumped, prompting a loud guffaw from a man seated nearby, when Orin's fist landed on top of the wooden bar so forcefully Ari expected to see it crack in two.

He backed up a step involuntarily as Orin stormed in his direction, head down like a bull. He hooked Ari's arm in a surprisingly gentle grip, pulling him alongside as he slammed out of the door. The fallen shutter clattered against the ground behind them.

Ari tried to read his expression, but Orin faced determinedly ahead, propelling them swiftly toward the docks. "Am I to assume that the service of a singer was unavailable in that establishment?"

Orin's mouth tightened at the corners as he adjusted his grip on Ari's arm. "Got some unfinished business I was hoping to leave behind, but it followed me here like a bad odor. Sorry I didn't get your song, sugar. We'll find another one after we hightail it out of here."

Ari pulled at his arm until he was released and glanced up and down the street to find no one had taken their notice. The crowd flowed around them like a rock in a stream.

Orin frowned down at him for only a moment before turning and heading toward their ship at as rapid a pace as he could manage without breaking into a trot.

Unfortunately, this forced Ari to actually break into a trot to keep up. The indignity of this kept him distracted from inquiring as to the rush to vacate the area.

Orin had already brought down the ramp and boarded the ship by the time Ari reached it, barking back a command to close the bay doors and begin takeoff procedures as Ari walked up the ramp.

"Gotta go, now. Faster is better than slower. Hold on to something, sweetheart. This might not be my smoothest waltz."

Ari hung onto the emergency stabilizing bars surrounding the bay doors as Orin initiated takeoff, lifting the ship from the ground as gracefully as ever. Just as they were able to break atmo without a tremor, Orin broke into colorful cursing, followed moments later by all hell breaking loose.

The ship lurched to the side, internal alarms blaring as Ari ran into the cockpit, careening off the walls as the ship shuddered and rolled.

Orin had already flung himself across the dash to fight the controls with both hands.

Ari buckled himself into the copilot's seat, trying to take in the clashing lights and alarms filling the cockpit. "What in the stars is happening?"

Orin's face was tight with strain, creative curses continuing to flow from between clenched teeth. "Delilah's been caught in a strangle net; can't get her free. Greasy bastard sold us out."

Ari watched helplessly as the wildly flashing emergency signals took over the dash, focusing on the insistently blinking red light above the ship's com. "We are being hailed. Shouldn't we answer?"

Orin's hand shot out to stop Ari from hitting the com. "It's Enforcers. Can't answer that until we get our story straight."

Ari's stomach dropped down to his toes, sweat breaking out across his forehead. "Oh dear. That is not ideal."

Orin snorted a laugh, amusement glinting across his eyes before they grew hard, determined. He hit the storage panel containing their pistols with the flat of one hand.

"This here ain't your weapon, understand? You never seen this shit before. You're an academic explorer who hired my seedy ass; easy to remember cause that's the truth. You don't know nothing 'bout nothing. They ask you about the Restricted Sector, you act real scared, you don't want no part of it, you would never attempt to breach it in your wildest dreams."

Ari sputtered, hands flailing in panic. "That's ridiculous, this was all my idea. Of course I shall stand up and take responsibility for any consequence which may ensue."

Orin's hand clapped down on the dash with a deafening crack of flesh against metal as the ship docked unsteadily, rocking them in their chairs.

"None of that shit, you hear me? You're an innocent Core professor and you been taken in by a shifty Verge rat, led astray. Worst-case scenario, they send you home. They'll be here any second now. You follow my lead and keep your trap shut. And, just in case things go south, it's been a real pleasure knowing you, Red."

Ari opened his mouth to ask how likely it was for that to happen when the bay doors screeched open from an external manual override.

Three Enforcers marched in, every movement perfectly synchronized and faces blank above their armored uniforms.

Ari watched in disbelief at the slow grin that spread across his partner's face, as Orin slowly unbuckled from his seat and moved to stand in the doorway between Ari and the line of Enforcers. His voice took on a mocking lilt Ari had never heard before.

"Well, how do you like that? Hey there, starlight, it's sure been a while."

The female Enforcer's face flashed with fury, her pointed chin rising as she fixed her glare and her weapon on Orin. He continued in his low drawl, completely unfazed by his hostile reception.

"But I forget my manners. Professor, allow me to introduce my wife."

Chapter Thirteen

Orin woke to the unfortunately familiar sensation of shackled wrists, groaning as he pulled himself out of his uncomfortable slump in the metal chair, shaking the numbness from his legs.

A thick set of mag-cuffs secured his hands in front of him, attached to a metal disk embedded in the concrete table. The shrill scrape of metal against metal grated in his ears as he shifted to take in his surroundings.

Most likely one of the lower-level interrogation chambers, little more than a concrete box. Orin not so fondly remembered the sparse decor. He smacked his mouth, trying to get rid of the cottony feeling that always lingered after a stun ray, and shivered against the persistent cold.

He swiveled his head to find the blinking red light in the uppermost corner, glaring at it for long minutes before blowing an exaggerated kiss.

Nothing for it now but to wait.

His thoughts turned to Aristotle, gut churning as he ran possible scenarios through his mind.

Where was the doctor?

Why had they been separated?

Had they set him free and kept Orin behind to address one or several of his warrants?

That last scenario was optimistic at best.

Still, Orin found himself hoping that Ari remained safe and unshackled somewhere far away from here. Man like that deserved better.

His musings were interrupted by the obnoxious buzzing sound of the metal door sliding open. Two Enforcers strode in to sit straight-backed in the chairs opposite the concrete slab he was tethered to.

He assessed them both, suppressing the unpleasant clenching sensation in his chest as he studied Isolde's face. Cataloged differences from the last time he had seen her, ignoring the twinge of curiosity over a new scar just above her upper lip.

Her fellow Enforcer was a study in opposites, broad where she was lithe, dark where she was pale. His unblemished skin and watchful eyes were the same deep shade of brown, his black curls cropped nearly down to the scalp. He appeared solid and respectable, posture ramrod straight and face impassive as he returned Orin's gaze unflinchingly.

He quickly shifted his gaze back to Isolde, her pale hair and skin striking against the blue of her uniform, just as beautiful as she was the miserable, soggy day of their wedding.

Leaning back in his chair, Orin sucked his teeth belligerently, lifted his chin in the direction of the male Enforcer.

"This your new man, little mouse?"

A muscle in her jaw twitched as she glanced at the man at her side and returned her focus to Orin. The glint of silver in her irises pulled at Orin. It was as if he were sinking into the mire of his past.

He hated it.

She inclined her head ever so slightly in the other Enforcer's direction.

"This is my partner, Enforcer Azu. We are here to ask you some questions regarding the circumstances under which you have been detained."

Against his will, Orin's mouth quirked up at the corners as he leaned forward on his elbows.

"Listen at you, girl. You have really made something of yourself. Looks like you did the right thing, dropping me like a shipment of manure three days late for delivery. I ain't even mad. Good for you. How'd you learn to talk like that?"

The corner of her mouth lifted slightly, her gaze slipping to the table between them, focusing on his shackled hands before lifting back to his face.

"What is the nature of your association with Dr. Campbell?"

He threw a particularly obnoxious smirk in her direction. "Well, now, a gentleman would never kiss and tell."

He waited a few silent beats under the cold stares directed his way, a drop of sweat running down the back of his collar.

"Where is he?" he asked, wincing internally at showing his hand.

"That is none of your concern. What is your relationship to Dr. Campbell?"

Orin weighed his options. A simple truth was always better than a lie if you could get away with it.

"I'm his pilot. Hired ship hand, that's all."

"Were you aware that you have been piloting a stolen vessel set on an unauthorized course past the Verge?" Enforcer Azu asked.

His voice was irritatingly as deep and smooth as his complexion. Orin found himself hoping the man had a patchy crop of back hair, at least. It wasn't fair for a man to be so obnoxiously flawless.

Orin cocked his head to the side, arranging his features in blinking innocence.

"Don't know nothing 'bout no stolen ship. But that wonky course, well, that's gotta be my mistake. I never had much schooling, see. All these fancy navigational calculations tend to tax my brainbox something fierce. Musta missed a number here or there to have gotten us so off course. I'll need to apologize to the professor. Ask him to double-check my numbers next time."

Isolde squinted at him.

"Enforcer Azu, I believe we will require both suspects in order to most effectively continue this interrogation."

Her partner stood and left the room, the buzzing of the door seeming to echo at his departure.

"Where's he—" Orin startled as Isolde grabbed his hand, delicate fingers biting into his palm.

"He's fetching your man," she hissed, "You have approximately three minutes to tell me what ridiculous scheme you have gotten yourself into before he gets back."

Now there was no stopping the surprised glee that split his face. "Knew you were still sweet on me."

She rolled her eyes, folding her arms across her chest in a familiar combative stance, lifting her chin in the direction of the door. "It's your professor who's sweet on you. Poor little thing's close to tears, demanding to know what we've done to you."

Orin's brow folded together with concern. "He's alright? You didn't hurt him, did you? He's done nothing wrong, swear on my mother's grave, Izzy. He's a good man. I'm sure you've got a pile of reasons to keep me here in chains, but you need to let him go."

Her pale face was assessing, scanning him over.

"You're as bad as each other. Your doctor will not be mistreated. You can drop your shoulders from your ears."

Orin did just that, he hadn't realized he had been lifting them in apprehension at the mention of Aristotle. "I'm serious now. I'm just a hired hand. He's a respectable Core scientist who wouldn't look twice at a thug like me."

Isolde smiled at that, a tiny little thing that curved her thin, pretty lips into a perfect bow. "Oh, I think he's looked more than twice. Poor man's besotted."

Orin tried to keep the joy from his face, but it was like trying to cover the sun with a handwoven basket.

Isolde blew a raspberry at him in disgust. "A stolen ship, Orin? Really? I know you lost your last one over a technicality, but—"

Orin snorted derisively. "A technicality, she says. It was Enforcer bullshit, stomping on Verge rats just to watch us squirm."

"—but I can't believe you would make an attempt to jump the Verge in a stolen ship! Smuggling a Core citizen! Where was your head?"

Orin lifted his gaze resolutely over her head. "Ain't stolen."

Isolde sighed, rolling her lips in her teeth the way she only did when she was losing patience.

"Is he really that good? Smuggling pure gold in those trousers or something? It's not like you to lose your head over a pretty face. They could put you away for this, you know. Your pretty little Core darling will get slapped with a fine and house arrest, but your giant Verge ass will get dumped in a hole, and you know it. So I'll ask you again. He worth it?"

Orin dropped his voice to a growl, squaring his jaw. "Ain't. Stolen."

They both turned at the hiss of the door. Orin sat up in his chair at the sight of Aristotle clapped in mag-cuffs too big for his slender wrists, stumbling after Enforcer Azu who had his elbow in an iron grip.

In a practiced movement, Azu pushed Ari down onto the chair beside Orin and secured his cuffs to the table with a metallic snap.

Orin's lips tried to twitch up as Ari sat with perfect posture, acting more like he was taking tea than enduring an interrogation.

Isolde had snapped back into her Enforcer face, blank and rigid in her chair as though she had never shown a hint of her former self.

Orin was as impressed as he was saddened to see it.

Enforcer Azu lifted an Enforcer-blue pad in his hands and passed it to Isolde silently. Her nose crinkled slightly as she read.

"The ship is registered to one Theo—Theoff—Theoffrass—"

Ari sighed deeply. "Theophrastus. Yes, I know."

Orin enjoyed the novelty of being the more compliant detainee for once in his life as Isolde continued with a quelling glance in Ari's direction.

"The ship is registered to one Theophrastus Campbell. Neither of whom are you."

Aristotle clucked his tongue impatiently, causing Orin to goggle at him in disbelief. Ari leaned in toward Isolde, ignoring the bulk of his cuffed hands on the table between them. "Theophrastus is my brother. The ship is registered in his name, but I am listed as secondary."

Isolde studied her pad.

"I don't have your name here. Sharing a last name proves nothing to me; Campbell isn't that uncommon."

Ari actually rolled his eyes. Orin tried not to swallow his tongue in terrified glee. And here he thought the professor couldn't get more attractive. If he kept on with this sassing of Enforcers, Orin was liable to get an indecency charge tacked on.

Ari attempted an impatient gesture, somehow managing to make the stilted movement of his cuffed hands appear elegant. "This is absurd. I demand that you pull up his ident and try to tell me he isn't my brother."

Orin knocked his knee against Ari's leg, earning an irritated frown as if he wasn't trying to save Ari's narrow ass from himself.

Isolde glared at Aristotle but tapped on her pad, huffing irritably until she froze in her seat. She lifted her head to scan over Ari's face.

"Damn."

Orin snorted as she shook herself back into Enforcer blankness with a subtle nudge at Enforcer Azu as she handed him the pad. He looked down, back up at Ari's face, then down again before tapping rapidly on the screen.

He kept his handsome face blank as he stared at Ari.

"Secondary registration. Aristotle Campbell."

Orin swallowed a whoop, turning it into a cough at an unamused glare from the Enforcers.

Aristotle settled back into his perfect posture, lacing his fingers together on the table like he had been the one to call this meeting. One delicate red brow rose imperiously.

"Indeed."

Orin couldn't contain it, mag-cuffs groaning as he shifted excitedly. "Told you that shit ain't stolen!"

Aristotle didn't even twitch. "My partner is correct."

Isolde's hand jerked slightly in the way that told Orin she would like nothing more than to rub her forehead in frustration. Her Enforcer training held, and her fingers remained tense against the table instead.

Enforcer Azu placed the pad on the table and rested his hands in an exact mirror of Isolde's.

All their perfect synchronization was starting to creep Orin out, tell the truth.

Enforcer Azu turned to face Ari in tiny precise motions like he was a dial turned two clicks to the left. "There remains the matter of your unauthorized course, Dr. Campbell. As the owner of the ship, responsibility falls to you."

Orin's wrists yanked against his cuffs as he forgot himself and attempted to stand.

"Hold up, now, I'm the rusted pilot! I set the course, so it's my responsibility. He's got nothing to do with it."

Ari's knee pressed solidly against Orin's leg, but he kept his face turned toward the Enforcers, somehow managing to show nothing more than slight irritation in his expression.

"What my partner means to say is that we are sure there has been some sort of misunderstanding. We are an exploratory vessel traveling along the Verge in order to collect geological samples for study. There would be no purpose to our traveling beyond the geological structures of the Verge settlements."

Enforcer Azu remained motionless, focused on Ari's face. "And yet we detected a plotted course for jumping the Verge."

Ari's face creased in a shockingly convincing display of confusion. "I'm afraid that makes no sense whatsoever. Perhaps it would be prudent to check the ship's navigational logs again."

Enforcer Azu didn't move except to blink once, which apparently signaled Isolde to grab the pad and start tapping away. Orin struggled to maintain his easy sprawl in his chair. Ari just kept his angelic little face trained on the Enforcers.

Isolde's forehead wrinkled in consternation as she tapped, paused, then tapped again more rapidly. She held the pad out to her partner, who finally broke his staring contest with Ari to read the screen. Orin was deeply satisfied to see his handsome face twist in irritation before he abruptly stood and stalked out of the room.

Orin turned to Isolde, mouth hanging open as Ari's cuffs suddenly released, the two empty halves clanking on the tabletop.

Isolde gave the tiniest sigh, ignoring Orin. "You and your vessel are free to go, Dr. Campbell. There appears to have been a computing error. I apologize for the inconvenience."

Ari didn't move except to fold his hands more precisely on the tabletop. "I am unable to travel properly without my pilot, Enforcer."

Orin's chest squeezed painfully at the words, part of him having expected Aristotle to get up and walk away without a second thought. He knew he wasn't exactly a big loss. Shipless pilots were a dime a dozen on the Verge. Ari could have another shifty bastard in his cockpit within the hour. The thought made Orin sick to his stomach.

Isolde's face remained carefully blank as she addressed Ari. "Mr. Stone still needs to clear up some issues with his licensing. He stays here until we have his paperwork in order."

"Excellent. Shall we proceed with due haste, then? One does have a certain expectation of efficiency as is so often proclaimed by the Academy." Ari sniffed disdainfully before cutting green eyes in Orin's direction.

Orin felt a slipping sensation as though he'd missed the last step off the ramp, but instead of hitting the ground, he just kept falling over and over and over again into those eyes.

Well, damn. So much for not getting attached.

Chapter Fourteen

Enforcer Azu returned momentarily and slid a sheaf of papers onto the table in front of Orin. Ari saw at a glance that it was a stack of legal documents, written by hand in the formal calligraphy customary of Core governmental documentation.

Orin regarded the documents as one might react upon finding a Zingarian warsnake in one's shoe.

Ari clasped his hands more firmly together atop the table, resisting the urge to smooth his fingers over the tense lines of Orin's back. The man sat like he was facing an ordeal far worse than paperwork, scanning the room as if searching for an escape route.

Enforcer Azu lifted the top sheet, barely glancing down at it before carefully watching the pair of them as he launched into a flat recitation of licensing requirements for a class A pilot. Ari tuned out after the first few phrases, allowing his attention to travel over the handsome Enforcer. He was large and solidly built, the broad line of his shoulders enhanced by his molded armor.

Ari had long acknowledged his preference for men of a certain size, and he couldn't help but notice that only days before, he would have considered the handsome Enforcer to be a perfect specimen.

Now, however, he could only note the smooth unblemished skin and perfectly symmetrical features, the unscarred hands carefully laying the document in the space between Orin and Ari. All of these things now seemed unappealing to Ari, who apparently preferred a bit more texture. Something very much like the large, marked-up hands that stuck out gracelessly from the set of cuffs still attached to the table.

The female Enforcer noticed Ari's attention to those hands, minutely raising a pale eyebrow before tapping on her pad and blanking her expression as the cuffs released and fell open with a dull *thunk*.

She swept both sets of cuffs off the table and attached them to her belt with a practiced click. Removing a polished chrome ink pen from some hidden pocket, she then placed it quietly on the slab in front of her.

Orin pulled his hands into his lap, rubbing his wrists absentmindedly. Ari noted angry red marks from the pressure of cuffs which were not built to contain a man of Orin's size.

Enforcer Azu was finally winding down his monotonous spiel when Orin brought his right index finger up to trace over a line of looping script, squinting in concentration before returning his hands to his lap and staring hard at the wall across from them.

The female Enforcer breathed a soft sound, stern expression breaking for a moment as she made an arrested motion toward the documents, which she quickly and ruthlessly suppressed. She then sat perfectly still beside her partner, who finally concluded his rote recitation of legalities. Both Enforcers watched Orin expectantly, a slight tinge of impatience beginning to crack the edges of Enforcer Azu's expression.

A ringing silence stretched across the concrete slab, interrupted only by the muted clatter of a small metal cap hitting the table as Orin picked up the pen. He proceeded to scan over the paper with a furrowed brow as he searched for the space to sign.

Aristotle cleared his throat and reached for the papers in an awkward flail of wrists and elbows, knocking the pen from Orin's hand to rattle onto the metal floor.

"As Mr. Stone's business partner, I will be reviewing all documentation prior to either of us signing any agreement, in the interest of full disclosure within our business venture."

He felt Orin's gaze burning the side of his face as he raised the first page and began to read aloud, pausing to request a glass of water after the seventh page. The female Enforcer left to retrieve it, and he continued on, gratefully accepting the glass when it appeared.

It was convoluted reading material, difficult to wade through and requiring the better part of an hour with breaks for sips of water.

Around midway through the documents, Ari felt a warm weight on his knee and glanced down to see that Orin had rested a broad hand there. Every few minutes, he would stroke the edge of Ari's kneecap with his thumb in an oddly soothing motion.

The strangest warmth filled Aristotle's chest cavity, like coming home to stand before the fire, only the fire was banked inside his rib cage. A truly peculiar sensation.

Peculiar and addictive.

*

Ari waited until the bay doors shut behind them before letting his knees turn to water, sliding down the wall to sit on the galley floor. Orin was already strapping into the pilot's seat and flicking the controls to prepare for takeoff. He practically vibrated with his need to get far away as soon as possible, large hands shaking minutely over the controls.

Ari stumbled over to the copilot's seat and buckled in just in time for Delilah's release from the Enforcer ship dock, engines kicking on with a plaintive whine.

Orin patted the dash soothingly. "I know, honey. They treated you rough. I'll make it up to you, pretty girl."

Ari found himself fighting a fit of the giggles at Orin's fond words, giddy at the relief of their release so sharp it went to his head like a glass of champagne. He turned his head at Orin fussing over the ship's controls. "I can't believe it worked! I am simply astounded by the power of a few well-placed filing errors. Truly, I never expected them to prove so effective when I was putting them into place."

Orin laughed, shaking his head as his fingers flew over the controls. "Never woulda thought that, between the two of us, you'd be the criminal mastermind."

Ari laughed along with him, buoyed by his good humor in the wake of near disaster. He kept on smiling as he asked the question that had been tickling at the back of his mind, too overwhelmed by panic to come forward until now.

"What did you mean when you said that Enforcer was your wife?"

Orin shrugged, busily working across the dash as his smile slipped away.

"Ex-wife. Name's Izzy. We were young and stupid and coming out of a real bad situation. Loving each other was just about the only thing we had going for us at the time. Didn't last too long, less than a year before she dropped me like a bad habit. Always knew she was too good for the likes of me. Real proud of how she turned out;

Enforcer Academy ain't nothing to sneeze at. Good to see her make something of herself without me weighing her down."

His eyes were careful on Ari, lids lowered in a way that would have seemed nervous on another man.

Ari turned to fiddle with the copilot controls without actually altering anything about their takeoff. "So, you're not. You're not like me, then. You like, or rather, you prefer. Women."

Now, Orin finally appeared uncomfortable, shoulders rolling as he kept his focus fixed on the controls, the both of them pretending this takeoff was requiring the utmost concentration.

"Don't have a preference really. I just like people."

A tightness crossed Ari's chest, and he refused to examine the feeling further, fumbling out his words in a rush. "I suppose I just never knew there were people who could choose. Who they... Who they wanted."

Orin's eyes flashed soft and wounded before returning determinedly to the dash. "I didn't choose any more than you did. Just how I am."

Contrition flooded Ari at the stiff way Orin guided the ship away from the Enforcers, mouth held tight. He dropped his pretense of working the controls to swivel his chair in Orin's direction, hands folded together in an effort to appear composed.

"I apologize. I'm afraid I still have much to learn. Thank you for always being patient with me. In all respects. I'm afraid I don't deserve it."

Orin made a rude noise out of the side of his mouth, attention remaining fixed on the controls. "You deserve better than I could ever give you, and that's a fact. Got nothing to do with the men and women in my past and everything to do with me and where I come from. Some places leave a stain so bad you can't never get clean of it. Doesn't matter what I can give you, anyway, cause you and I got a deadline on this thing between us."

Ari nodded, firmly tamping down on the rolling in his gut. He knew as well as Orin that their relationship was temporary by necessity. Ari's focus had to remain on saving his brother. He understood that Orin's focus needed to stay fixed upon securing his ship.

It was good for them to be transparent about these things. Ari could not afford to become too attached, even as he ignored the alarm bells in his chest that signified such a thing might have already come to pass.

They settled into a course toward the next settlement on the list. Orin barely waited to check the autopilot before shoving out of the cockpit to go bang around in the storage panels of the main compartment.

Ari followed cautiously, watched as Orin lifted out a large metal crate before kicking the storage panel closed in a way that left Ari repressing his urge to check for dents.

Orin dropped the crate onto the floor with a concerning metallic crash.

"I'm not—" He ran one hand through his hair before gripping it in frustration.

"I can read. Alright? I can make out most things in standard block, just not that loopy shit you see on fancy docs like that. I know I'm not the brightest bulb on the dash, but I don't want you going around thinking I'm a complete idiot." He crossed his arms over the broad expanse of his chest, holding himself tightly.

Something in Ari's chest ached. His fingers itched to smooth the line that had formed between Orin's brows, but he folded his fingers together in front of himself to curb the impulse.

"You are one of the most intelligent men I have ever worked with, Mr. Stone. I have witnessed you perform calculations in your head that would have any professor of mathematics at my university reaching for the chalk."

Orin shook his head, clenching his hands around the sharp corners of his elbows. "That's just because numbers come easy to me. Numbers just make sense, is all."

Ari stepped close enough to pool the heat of their bodies in the space between them. He tilted his head up to Orin's face. "You are brilliant, and I will not entertain any argument to the contrary."

Orin stared down at him like he had been cracked open. His eyes shimmered with emotion threatening to spill over with every breath.

Aristotle found himself unwilling to resist the impulse to cup his hand over a darkly stubbled cheek. "Brilliant."

Orin turned into the caress, his breath shuddering across Ari's palm.

The world tilted, and for a fraction of a second, Ari worried that the ship had run into trouble. But, instead, Orin had swept him up into his arms, and his heavy boot heels now banged an urgent rhythm across the floor panels as he carried him into his bunk.

Chapter Fifteen

Ari bounced onto the mattress like a particularly delicate sack of potatoes.

"Off. Everything off," Orin grunted.

Orin's voice was muffled by the shirt he was wrestling over his head, braces already hanging in loops by his hips and trousers undone.

Ari rushed to comply as Orin's face emerged, full lips parted around heavy breath and eyes hot enough to set Ari's blood boiling in his veins.

He struggled out of his boots and waistcoat, just starting to unwind his ascot when big hands hooked into his waistband and yanked him across the bed. Orin tugged his trousers off without bothering with the fastenings. The harsh scrape of canvas down Ari's hips and thighs only served to sensitize his skin, every nerve ending wide awake and screaming for attention.

Ari redoubled his efforts, removing his shirt at record speed as Orin made quick work of his drawers. His hands slowed as he took in the sight of Ari splayed across the bed in only his stockings, one thick finger working under his right garter until the silk ribbon bit into the soft flesh of Ari's thigh.

Orin's tongue traced the length of his bottom lip as he drank in Ari carefully untying his garters and rolling down his stockings. His lips worked around words that remained mostly silent, a few escaping here and there in a roughly whispered litany of filthy praise.

Ari's gaze caught on the thick length of Orin's cock protruding from his open trousers, gleaming wet at the tip. He reached out before the thought was fully formed and wrapped his hands around it with a soft squeeze. Orin fell onto his elbows above him with a groan, kicking his trousers off the rest of the way.

The muscles of his arm bulged in a manner Ari would definitely be revisiting in his memory as Orin worked an arm under his back and lifted him to the center of the bed.

Orin's kiss was deep and urgent and yet so achingly gentle Ari felt raw from it. Words and emotions that had no place in their situation welled up inside him until his entire body ached with the effort of containing it all.

Orin kept his focus on him, his face filled to the brim with answering emotion, teeth clenched against the words that spilled out of him in staccato bursts of reluctant poetry.

Ari arched into the work-rough hands that ran up and down his torso as Orin dipped his head to lick at his small pink nipples, his eyes flashing up at him when Ari gasped against the pull of teeth.

Ari wove his fingers through the soft waves of Orin's hair, then caught and pulled, earning a startled grunt as Ari used his hold to pull Orin's face back up to his.

Ari's kiss had all of the depth and urgency of Orin's with none of the gentleness, abandoning soft licks to bite at Orin's lips and suck hard around his tongue when it emerged to erase the sting.

The sound Orin made at that hit Ari's bloodstream like a drug, sending him writhing and frantic, hands scratching down Orin's back and up through the hair across his chest.

Orin pushed up onto his elbows, bruised lips slick. Ari stretched to lick at them until Orin pinned him down with a gentle hand that spanned his chest from nipple to nipple.

"Alright, now. You're gonna burn a hole clean through my bed like this. Why don't you just tell me what you need? Anything you want, beautiful."

Ari twisted, lifting his hips to rub his cock against Orin's stomach until Orin held him firmly against the bed with the opposite hand on his hip. He whined against the immobility but something released inside him at the sensation of security all the same.

He tilted his head up to meet Orin's patient gaze as he slid his hands restlessly up the length of Orin's arms to hook over his shoulders.

"I just. I wish I could. I want to be closer to you. Even. Even closer than we are now, if that were possible."

Orin's eyes flared with heat. His voice dropped low to rumble all the way through Ari's bones to settle somewhere beneath his rib cage. "We could, if you wanted. Do you know, baby? Tell me you know. I could be all the way inside you, right here."

He dropped his hand between Ari's thighs, the soft weight of Ari's testicles lifted by his thick wrist as the rough pad of Orin's finger gently nudged over the entrance to his body. Ari gasped and writhed, unsure if he was trying to escape or get closer. Orin added the tiniest amount of pressure to his fingertip before he took his hand away, returning it to Ari's hip unconcernedly as if he had not just turned Ari's brain inside out.

Orin carefully regarded Ari's shocked face.

"Now, we don't gotta do nothing you don't wanna do. There's nothing I need from you but for you to tell me what you want. I got no expectations, alright?"

Ari nodded distractedly and pushed up against the hand holding his hips with a whine.

Orin kissed the tip of his nose. "Good. Now why don't you tell me what you want, gorgeous?"

Ari wrapped his arms around Orin's neck and tugged him down to nibble on the stubble lining his jaw. Orin hummed contentedly as Ari mumbled against the soft skin behind his ear.

"What's that, baby?"

Ari pulled back to look Orin in the eye.

"Everything. I said I wanted everything."

Orin's nostrils flared as his hands shifted and tightened their grip on Ari's body.

"Fuck yes. I'm gonna make you lose your rusted mind, sugar."

Ari was busy thinking of a retort to that when Orin broke free of his hold and dropped down to kneel between Ari's spread knees.

The skin of Orin's palms might have been rough, but his grip on Ari's thighs was softer than silk as he slowly urged them farther open, broad thumbs gliding up behind Ari's knees to bring them close to his chest.

"Can you hold these up for me, beautiful?"

Ari might have breathed an affirmative answer, but he couldn't hear himself over the thundering rush of his own heartbeat as he slipped trembling hands behind his knees. He transcended the need to blink when Orin leaned down to lay a burning trail of kisses along the back of his thighs, his hands framing Ari's ass.

Ari let out a strangled gasp when Orin swept his tongue over the sensitive patch of skin behind his testicles, the scratch of stubble rough and sweet along his crease as he kissed his way down and down and down, until...

There.

Orin kissed Ari's hole the same way he kissed his mouth, with devoted attention and a forceful mastery softened around the edges by his innate gentleness.

He eased back, red-faced and panting, to check on Ari.

"This alright?"

Ari nodded, choking hopelessly around the words he wanted to say, pleas and promises tangling together in his throat.

Orin seemed to hear them anyway, dimples popping before he dipped his head back down.

Ari's entire focus narrowed to the tiny knot of muscle as Orin's tongue traced secret patterns over and around and—Oh, Stars!—in. Ari opened around his tongue as Orin pressed relentlessly against him, slick and strong and inescapable. He worked him in an alternating rhythm of firm and fluttering strokes, pushing in and sucking back until Ari was floating.

His legs started to shake, the skin behind his knees growing slick with sweat as he struggled to hold them up with unsteady hands.

Orin sat up on his knees to suck his finger into his mouth. He observed Ari's face as he lowered his hand down to where Ari was slick and open from his kisses, guiding the tip of his finger just inside.

"You want this, sweetheart? You want me inside you?"

Ari didn't nod so much as toss his head wildly against the pillows, voice gone so high and breathy he didn't recognize himself. "Yes. You. Just you. Orin. Please."

Something shuddered through Orin at that, licking flames into his eyes as they dropped down from Ari's face to study what he was doing with the kind of focus Ari had only witnessed him devoting to the ship's controls.

Orin cupped his ass with both hands, curving his thumbs around to spread him open, and Ari could do nothing but blush to the roots of his hair. "Gorgeous," Orin whispered in a voice that should have been reserved for sacred temples or fervent prayers. A voice that smoothed along Ari's nerves like a tonic, pushing air into his lungs and filling in his hollow places.

Orin's hands gently lowered Ari's legs to rest against the mattress, petting over his thighs before Orin tilted off to the side and fished one arm for something under his bunk.

He emerged with a string-wrapped parcel. Ari had noticed it in their first port, and he pushed up onto his elbows as Orin carefully unwrapped one of the smaller parcels contained within. He exposed a simple bottle of clear fluid and tucked the rest of the package away under the bed.

The bottle was quickly forgotten as Orin crawled up the bed to rock his hips against Ari's, framing and surrounding him with the breadth of his shoulders as he dropped to lay a kiss on his lips that could have been sweet if Ari hadn't lifted to meet him with the full force of his enthusiasm.

Orin wove firm fingers through his hair, anchoring him and directing him into deeper, softer kisses until they were forced to pause for breath.

Ari wrapped his legs around Orin's hips, lifting and tilting until the hot length of Orin's cock slotted in his crease. Orin raised up for a better view of Ari's face as he moved his hips, sliding over and back until he caught against Ari's rim, both of them breathing harshly at the sensation.

Ari bared his throat with a low keen as Orin drifted his lips down the exposed vulnerability, shifting his hips to drag and catch again and again.

"Please," Ari said, digging his fingertips into the bunching muscle of Orin's arms.

Orin's chest rumbled against Ari's rib cage with the depth of his groan. "Again. Say it for me again, beautiful."

Ari hitched his heels up higher, digging into Orin's ass insistently. "Please. Oh, please. Oh, pl—"

He cut off with a strangled cry as Orin's fingers worked against his opening. Orin lifted onto his knees and elbow, the opposite hand cupping Ari's head to keep his face trained on him.

"You tell me if it's too much, sweetheart."

Ari simply moaned, shoving himself onto his fingers as much as he could. Orin's eyes were a glowing halo of amber around the black of his pupil as he circled his wet finger, easing in and pulling back by tiny increments until Ari was a babbling, begging mess.

The lid of the bottle clicked softly as Orin drizzled more of the fluid down Ari's crease before his finger was back, gliding in more firmly this time until Ari had taken him down to the last knuckle.

Ari's hands clawed at his shoulders as he stared up at him incredulously. "Orin, you. You're inside me," he said before his brain could stop spinning long enough to worry about sounding like an idiot.

It was worth it for the pleased smile that bloomed across Orin's face, slow and sweet and sharp enough to split Ari right in half.

"That's right. Do you like it? Want more, baby?"

Ari's affirmations were such that they left no room for uncertainty regarding his enthusiasm. Orin laughed breathlessly as he twisted his finger, corkscrewing in and out and back in again in a building rhythm that took over Ari's every thought.

He was panting, mouth open and spilling out sounds he never knew he was capable of when Orin's second finger nudged against his opening with another click of the lid. This time, there was a sting with the careful invasion. Ari sucked in a harsh breath and reached down to wrap one hand around Orin's wrist as he paused at the second knuckle.

"Okay, beautiful? You still with me?"

Ari squeezed his wrist in reassurance, swallowing hard before he could answer.

"Yes. Oh, yes. Please don't stop."

Orin leaned in to kiss him, his talented tongue working to distract him as his fingers inched all the way inside. They fell back into that rhythm, the sting fading as Orin stretched him carefully with his thick fingers. Ari already felt so full he couldn't imagine how he would feel when he was truly—Oh!

He cried out, mind blanking with bliss as Orin brushed something inside him that sent sparks of pleasure shooting up his spine.

Ari blinked everything back into focus at Orin's pleased chuckle.

"There it is. You like that?"

Ari nodded, hands scrabbling at Orin's shoulders as his fingers carefully and precisely found that spot again, rubbing little circles that had Ari squirming with incoherent moans.

Orin panted as though he had been gut-punched, jaw dropped and chest heaving as he divided his attention equally between Ari's face and the place where his fingers disappeared.

"Gorgeous. Look at you. You were made for this."

Ari pushed back onto his fingers, earning a direct jab to that spot that left his thighs shaking and toes curling into the sheets, his rough cry echoing against the metal wall panels.

Orin's eyelids slid to half-mast.

"Just like that, sweet thing. Show me how you want it."

Ari pushed back again and again, breath catching as the tip of Orin's third finger nudged alongside the first two still working inside him.

Orin brushed his lips against Ari's knee, voice dragging low and ragged around the edges. "I know, baby. You want me to stop here? We can finish just like this."

Ari shook his head frantically, moaning his distress as he impaled himself on Orin's fingers. Orin retreated until just two fingertips rested inside, slowly rubbing and stretching around his rim. Ari took a calming breath, hands gripped hard into the firm strength of Orin's arms.

"Please don't stop. It just. It just feels like a lot. To. To. To take."

Orin stole a quick kiss, nudging their noses together affectionately.

"I know it is, sweetheart. Thing is, I ain't exactly a small man, and I'll be damned if I'm gonna hurt you. Takes a while to get you ready for me, nice and proper. And if we're gonna do this, I'm doing it proper. Just the way you deserve."

Ari nodded, rubbing their cheeks together. He then reached down to guide Orin's hand more firmly against him, taking another deep breath to try to force himself to relax.

This time, Orin hooked his fingertips into Ari's rim, pulling him open slowly and gently before ducking to lick around his fingers as they slid back in, all three tucked together into a gradually widening wedge.

Ari closed his eyes against the sting, fingers petting through the messy waves of Orin's hair that tickled against his thighs. His eyes shot open again at the first touch of Orin's tongue to his neglected cock as he lapped up the sticky mess Ari had been steadily leaking onto his stomach.

"Oh. Oh my. Orin!"

Orin glanced up at him, amber sparkling beneath dark lashes as he licked a wide stripe up the underside of Ari's aching cock, fingers pushing and twisting inside of him.

His knuckles rubbed over that sweet spot just as he sucked at the head of Ari's cock, and Ari tumbled over the edge, crying out and spilling down Orin's throat as he swallowed without a hint of hesitation or surprise.

He pulled off with a pop, fingers beginning to retreat until Ari shot his hand down to wrap around Orin's wrist, keeping him firmly in place.

"No. Stay. I'm sorry. I didn't mean to. Please don't stop."

Orin wavered, face flushed with a sheen on his lips. He painted an absolutely edible picture, and Ari was determined to have all of him. He held Orin's hand tightly against his body, gasping at the shockwaves of overstimulation. Orin chewed on his swollen lips as his focus locked between Ari's legs. He shook his head minutely, gaze flicking up to Ari's face before falling back down as though drawn by a magnet.

"I don't want to hurt you, baby."

Ari risked letting go of Orin's wrist to run his hands up his arms and neck until he framed his face, stubble rubbing harsh against his palms.

"It's fine. It's good. I want. I want you inside me. Please."

Orin's eyes clenched shut at the last word, breath shuddering hard between parted lips.

He propped himself on his elbow, cupping Ari's head and tangling their gazes into an inescapable knot as his fingers started to move slowly and carefully, avoiding that spot as Ari shivered every time he drew near. Orin's fingers spread Ari open until he was taking all three of them as easily as he had taken one.

To Ari's shock, his cock remained hard, flushed and throbbing insistently as though he had never spilled. Orin noticed this with a soft laugh, kissing him gently and whispering directly into Ari's ear.

"You're a star-dusted miracle, sweetheart. Never seen something so good."

Ari's resultant shiver had little to do with the careful motion of Orin's fingers and everything to do with the rough sweet sound of his voice, running through his hidden places like a caressing hand.

Orin worked him for long minutes punctuated by soft kisses and mumbled praise until the jagged edge of oversensitivity faded away, and Ari pushed back in a desperate attempt to rub Orin's fingers over that amazing spot.

Orin did just that with a cheeky grin as Ari's whole body jolted into the sensation. He stopped to pick up the forgotten bottle and clicked it open softly to slick himself up with a fraction of the care he'd shown Ari.

His slippery hand smoothed much more gently over Ari's cock, barely lingering long enough to get him wet before grabbing onto Ari's hip.

"You ready for me, beautiful?"

Open and empty and desperate to be filled, Ari already ached for the memory of Orin's fingers moving inside of him. His response was a garbled mess of "yes" and "please" and Orin's name, but Orin reacted as though he had spouted poetry, honey eyes wide and worshipful.

His body formed a canopy over Ari's as he settled into the cradle of his hips, angling Ari's legs high along his sides before sliding his forearms beneath Ari's shoulders, big hands framing Ari's head until he had no choice but to return his steady gaze.

"Alright, sweetheart?"

Ari brushed their lips together, breathing his answer more than giving it voice.

"Please."

Orin held his gaze as he eased his hips forward, both of them sighing in relief when his blunt tip breached Ari without too much resistance. Ari's relief was short lived as he kept on, the thick length of his cock far surpassing the stretch of his fingers.

Orin paused and pulled almost all the way back out before pushing in a tiny bit farther than he had before. He continued this careful invasion until their pelvises finally met, Ari panting through his nose against the sting.

It seemed as though Orin was having similar difficulty maintaining his composure, sweat dotting his brow and muscles jumping.

"Baby. Tell me you're okay."

Ari reached for words, opening and closing his mouth a few times before he could force them out.

"Yes. You. You're so big."

Orin winced and rolled his shoulders in as if that could possibly help him seem smaller.

"I know, sweetheart. I'm sorry. Is it too much? Want to stop?"

Ari smoothed his hand over Orin's jaw, gently working free the lip Orin held between his teeth with his thumb.

"It's perfect. You're perfect."

Orin's face was as raw as Ari felt, searing itself into his memory until Orin dropped his head to nuzzle into Ari's neck, eyelashes damp and fluttering against Ari's throat.

Ari stroked over the knobs of his spine as he wrapped his legs higher around him. He tilted his hips experimentally and drew in a harsh breath as Orin slid impossibly deeper.

Orin pulled back out slowly, giving Ari a moment before edging back in at the same glacial pace. The silken drag of him against Ari's insides was so different from the roughness of his fingers, Ari was captivated instantly by the sensation.

Orin kept moving at that pace, shifting his hips slightly each time. On the next surge forward, he rubbed his entire length along that spot, and Ari saw stars. Orin groaned at the involuntary clench of Ari's body before picking up his pace with even, measured strokes to graze against him just right while focused on each shift of Ari's face.

The soreness of his entry had faded, but it never went away completely, the tiny edge of pain somehow brightening the pleasure in ways Ari could never have imagined.

The stretched, full feeling was as unexpectedly delightful as that first blunt press of Orin's cock to the back of his throat had been, and equally addictive.

Ari licked the sweat from Orin's throat and lifted his hips into every thrust, abandoning himself completely. The sounds spilling from his own throat should have sent him blushing, but instead, he reveled in the deep, dark noises he elicited from Orin in response.

Grunts and groans cut with words so sweet they melted into Ari's sweat-slick skin, soaking into all of his layers until he was saturated by the feeling of Orin covering him inside and out.

"So good. You take me so good, beautiful. Never. I never. Gorgeous, just gorgeous. Stars, look at you."

Orin's voice was wrecked, dipping low and rough with a resonant growl.

Ari shivered at the sound and rolled his hips, crying out as the motion dragged his slick cock over the ridges of Orin's hardworking abdomen, the friction sending him careening closer to the edge with every perfect thrust.

Orin's heavy-lidded gaze honed in on some hint in Ari's face as he leaned on one elbow to reach between their bodies. He wrapped his hand around Ari's cock, working him in time with his thrusts.

Ari was already there by the time Orin slicked his broad thumb over the head of his cock, and his legs jerked against Orin's sides as he spilled onto both of their chests with a shout.

"Perfect. Like that. Just like that, sweetheart."

The wet slide of their bodies added to the obscene sounds in the room. Orin pressed his lips to Ari's throat with a deep moan and thrust faster and harder until he filled Ari up with hot pulses deep inside him.

Ari's arms tightened around Orin as he collapsed for just a moment, the solid weight of him satisfying something Ari didn't know he had been starving for.

Orin took a moment to catch his breath before kissing Ari with trembling lips. He stroked Ari's thighs as he carefully pulled out with a shift of his hips.

Ari hissed at the loss, the sting rising fresh and raw as he was left feeling open and bereft, clenching around nothing.

Orin's face creased with concern, and he pushed up onto his knees to spread Ari's thighs apart and peer down into the mess between his legs. Ari covered his face in mortification at Orin's release leaking out of him onto the bedsheets.

Gentle fingertips brushed over his sore hole, Orin inspecting with close attention, and Ari peeked between his fingers. Orin hummed thoughtfully before sitting back with a decisive nod, allowing Ari to close his legs in a last-ditch effort to preserve his dignity.

"You're alright, baby. Just let me clean you up, and you'll feel better."

Ari didn't have a chance to respond before Orin disappeared into the en suite. He returned with a damp cloth that he held carefully to Ari's crease, instantly soothing the sting. Making quick work of cleaning them both, he tossed the cloth onto the floor. He climbed back in bed to gather Ari into his arms and tug the blanket up over their hips.

Ari turned to lay his head against the broad muscle of Orin's chest. Squeezing his eyes shut, he feigned sleep as he listened to Orin's heart and administered a stern dressing down to his own, which seemed intent on leaping into a depth of emotion entirely unsuitable for their situation.

His heart responded with a defiant thump when Orin brushed gentle lips over the top of his head and whispered softly into his hair, wishing him the sweetest of dreams.

Chapter Sixteen

Orin struggled to keep the guilty pride from his face as Ari sat in the copilot's chair with exaggerated care, a rosy blush staining his cheeks when he glanced in Orin's direction.

Tearing himself away to focus on the view screen, Orin flicked switches that didn't really alter anything about their landing, just to appear busy. He accidentally hit one that could have altered their trajectory but swiftly flicked it back with a muttered curse and a fervent apology to Delilah for his stupidity and distraction.

Could hardly blame a man for being stupid when he had someone like Ari peeking up at him from under his lashes like that. Orin felt like he'd left his brain in a puddle on his bedroom floor next to a discarded set of garters.

Ari waited patiently until Orin had completed docking procedures before commanding his attention with a small cough.

"Are we going to speak with another singer?"

Orin pushed up from his seat, barely resisting the urge to cup Ari's face in his palm and, instead, skimmed his hand over the top of his slicked-back hair in an awkward sort of pat.

Ari gave him a quizzical expression at that, smoothing his own hair in place as he stood to follow.

Orin started up the ramp before turning to answer. "Sure we are, sugar. Right after we hit the firing range.

Gotta teach you to fend for yourself out there after you fetch your brother and I'm not around no more."

He threw Ari what he'd need in an underhanded toss, and Ari fumbled to catch the little garter pistol, giving Orin time to rearrange his face and wipe away the melancholy that welled up at the thought of leaving Ari. He shook himself sternly as he stomped down the ramp. No point dwelling on the inevitable. He'd have plenty of time to cry into his beer after he served his purpose and little Red kicked his ass to the curb. He could cry into his beer on his own damn ship, in fact.

*

Big Blaster's firing range was as shabby as they come, all the paint chipping off the walls and targets riddled with laser burns, but Orin knew it to be safe despite all appearances. Well-maintained enough to keep the blasts contained and away from the customers.

Ari eyed the ramshackle booth dubiously when they stepped inside.

"May not look like much, but the place is solid," Orin reassured him, banging on the wall with his fist and wincing as one of the acoustic panels broke off and fell to the floor at their feet.

Ari rolled skeptical eyes up at him, pretty lips pressed into a thin line against what Orin was sure would be a blistering opinion of the premises.

Orin kicked the panel away discreetly as he stepped up beside Ari to align his shoulders and feet in demonstrating proper shooting procedure.

Orin held up his laser pistol and hit the center of the target with lazy precision, being sure to keep himself in tight position as he narrated everything he was doing for

Ari. He then stepped back and gestured to him forward to give it a go.

Ari lifted his adorable pistol dutifully, pale hand steady as he supported his wrist with the opposite forearm just as instructed. Orin suppressed a grin at the tip of his little pink tongue peeking out of the corner of his mouth as he squinted in concentration.

Ari took a deep breath before pulling the trigger, and green lights flashed through their booth as the stun ray hit the target dead center.

Orin's grin could no longer be suppressed. "You're a natural, sweetheart. Nothing to it, right?"

Ari shifted his feet, a hint of green flashing up and then back down to the weapon in his hands. "I suppose it is a useful skill to cultivate if I am to get through the deep dark."

Orin snorted, adjusting Ari's stance before gesturing for him to try again.

"Round here, it's a useful skill for skipping to the corner store. Can't be too careful on the Verge, Red, remember that."

*

The smell of the saloon hit like a drunkard's fist as soon as a man wandered out of the door. Orin stifled a laugh at Ari's offended expression, cute little nose wrinkled up against the stench. He leaned in close, ruffling his silky red hair with his nose, hand skimming over the sway of Ari's lower back.

"Stick around long enough, and you'll get used to it, sugar."

Ari cast him a doubtful glance, hand hovering over his ascot as though he were debating bringing it up to cover his nose. Orin kind of hoped he would, if only for the picture he would make.

He hardened his face into a practiced smirk as they approached the dented metal bar. Dripping rust stains marred the entire stretch, disappearing into the filthy concrete floor under the mismatched stools. Orin chose the cleanest one in the bunch to perch Ari onto before leaning over the bar to signal for a drink.

The barkeep turned in his direction, gray hair floating off in all directions around his head like it couldn't be bothered to abide by the laws of gravity.

Orin tapped the bar twice with his knuckles, and, quick as a lick, the barkeep brought over two glasses of beer. Foam sloshed onto the bar top as he set them down, the liquid following the dripping rust lines of untold numbers of previous libations. Ari sniffed at his beer before pushing it away discreetly.

Orin called the retreating barkeep back with a low whistle. The well-worn skin of the keep's forehead collapsed into accordion folds as he lifted bushy eyebrows in Orin's direction. Orin leaned over the bar, voice lowered.

"Might be, I'm listening for a singer. Who's on the wind tonight?"

The barkeep gave the room a sweep, shiny eyes rolling like marbles under the folds of his brow. When he drew closer in to answer, his breath nearly knocked Orin back a pace, seeming to solve the mystery of the stench all on its own.

"Might be I know a song or two, stranger. Name's Amos, if you're listening. Hear anything you like, and I can put it on your tab."

Orin nodded, twisting his glass on the bar top with one hand as he got Ari's attention by dropping the other to his thigh with a squeeze.

"Alright, Amos. You got a song for Red over here? Seen him around or heard tell of someone like him out here?"

Amos squinted at Ari, considering. Orin felt the need to check for smoke coming out of his ears, the poor man's brain was working so hard. Amos scanned Ari up and down as Ari sat up straight on his stool, hands carefully resting away from the wet spot on the bar.

"Yeah, sure, I seen him. Last time he was here, he was playing grab ass with some other fella, sorry to tell it, stranger. Odd kinda man, real shifty. Like, couldn't look at you 'less it was sideways. The other guy, not your little strawberry tart. All inked up the way Outliers are sometimes. Big 'un too. Not near as big as you though. But I ain't never come across none as big as you."

Orin debated pulling up a stool of his own to watch as Ari folded his hands at his waist, acting for all the world as if he was preparing to enter a spirited scholarly discussion. He winced as Ari's posture grew so erect he could've been a marble column formed entirely of disapproval and affront.

"That 'tart' you are referring to is my brother, Theo. And he was not playing grab anything. He was being held against his will. By that man."

Amos' eyes widened incredulously, rolling over Ari from head to toe with a blatant disregard for his deepening scowl. "Well, I'll be damned. Spitting image, ain't you? Think he was in over his head with that odd fella? That's a shame. Though, truth to tell, it looked the other way round, to me."

Ari opened his mouth to unleash what was sure to be a vicious retort, but Orin put pause to that by laying his hand gently on Ari's arm, giving Amos his attention.

"Reckon so? How do you figure?"

Amos scratched the overgrown patch of gray whiskers on his chin thoughtfully.

"Looked to me like strawberry tart was doing all the talking, leading tall dark and creepy around by the nose. Man was more like a shadow, just looming over his shoulder all night."

To Orin's fascination, Ari's face contorted into a pained expression, delicate fingers lifting to pinch the bridge of his nose as he shook his head with a quiet groan. Orin leaned in, keeping his voice low. "You alright, sweetheart?"

The groan gained volume at the same rate at which it gained consonants and vowels, morphing into a long drawn out "Thhhhheeeeeeooooooooo!"

Ari dropped his hand, clenching it into a fist as he muttered darkly. "Of all the—of course he would— I cannot believe this!"

Orin leaned back, still keeping his voice low. "You, uh, you alright, honey?"

Amos took the opportunity to wander away, drying a glass with a stained rag as he turned his attention to another patron.

Orin steered Ari to a table in the corner, keeping the wall at their backs with a good view of the door. When Ari dropped his head to the table without voicing a single concern for the cleanliness, Orin's concern immediately doubled. He rubbed Ari's back soothingly.

"Okay, baby. So we know he was here; that's good. That's something to go on. Seems he was doing just fine, too, to hear Amos tell it."

Ari lifted his head and cuddled back into Orin's arm, nodding thoughtfully.

"You're right. Of course, you're right. This is a good thing. For just a moment, I was afraid— You have been telling me all of this time that he had simply run away, and I never believed it. But no; I know my brother. He left that note. It is clearly an abduction."

Orin nodded sympathetically, cupping his hand around Ari's shoulder. A man at the next table turned to them with a snide leer, and Orin offered his best menacing stare, casually exposing his firearm with a shift of his coat. The man hastily found something fascinating at the bottom of his glass.

Ari scrubbed his hands over his face fitfully. "The thing is. My brother. He isn't— He's not like me."

Orin made a vague gesture with the index finger of both hands that he immediately regretted. "You mean, like with men?"

Ari turned to goggle at him, as if Orin had suddenly developed a crisp Britannia accent. Fair enough, after that unfortunate gesture.

He shook his head slowly. "No. Not with. No. If anything, Theo has always been more accepting of that aspect of his nature."

Orin nodded, rolling his fingers into fists to keep them in check.

Ari continued, "I simply mean that Theo has what our mother always liked to call 'the gift of gab.' It would be fair to say Theo couldn't keep his mouth shut to save his life. But, perhaps— Perhaps his inability to keep quiet has helped him through this ordeal, if what the barkeep was saying is true."

Orin considered this as he draped his arm over Ari's slumped shoulders. "Sounds about right. Must have a mighty big brain in his head if he's anything like you. Using all he's got as best he's able."

Aristotle pulled at the cuff of Orin's coat, face downcast. "Do you— Do you think that he— After everything he said, about—about grabbing, do you think Theo has been forced to—to trade his virtue for his safety?" He lifted wounded eyes up to Orin.

Orin could say from experience that he would rather have faced the business end of a shotgun. Those baby greens ought to be illegal, glistening up at a man and seeming twice their size all of a sudden. Should think twice before swinging eyes like that around.

Might break something. Like Orin's stupid heart.

He sighed, tucking Ari's head into his shoulder and kissing his forehead, inhaling the herbal scent of his pomade. "I hope not, sugar. I surely hope not."

Orin really didn't want to tell him what he thought. Knowing what he did about the world of men, it was damn hard to be optimistic about a situation like that. But if Aristotle Campbell was getting beaten down by reality, it wasn't going to be Orin that dealt the final blow.

Chapter Seventeen

Ari shifted nervously in place on the galley bench as Orin walked into the room, smiling at him. He then noticed what was on the table and his prominent brow furrowed in confusion.

"Those are—" Orin tilted his head closer. "—kid's books, yeah?"

Ari sat straight-backed in his seat, hands folded over the open pages in front of him, unconsciously mimicking the posture of his favorite tutor.

"They are some of my childhood favorites, yes. I retrieved them from my brother's collection."

Orin slid onto the bench opposite him, honey eyes soft on Ari's face. "Why're you reading kid's books? You missing your brother, sweetheart?"

Ari cleared his throat, adjusting the book minutely as if to better align the edges with the tabletop. "I thought that perhaps we—perhaps— We could read them. Together. You and I. These editions were published in Core script. I thought they might be beneficial. For—for you."

Orin's bench screeched discordantly as he reared back from peering at the pages. "They're for me?"

Ari nodded slowly, carefully watching the storm brewing in his partner's face.

Orin's mouth worked for a moment before his words gritted out past his clenched teeth.

"You thought you could, what? Play teacher with me? Teach the filthy Verge rat to read? Trying to pretty up some of my rough edges?"

Ari reached across, his fingers barely making contact with the wide back of Orin's hand before it was wrenched away. He resolutely maintained eye contact despite the daggers being thrown in his direction.

"I thought to propose an exchange of skills, so that the both of us might be better equipped at the end of our association."

The thought of Orin being forced to navigate Core paperwork on his own after Aristotle was reunited with Theo kept haunting him. He could not push it from his mind.

Orin's face twisted into a smirking mask, one broad thumb reaching up to pull suggestively at his full bottom lip. "Here I thought I've been teaching you all kinds of skills. Didn't know I should've been angling for a trade."

Something hardened in his eyes as he looked at Ari, something brittle and sharp, glinting like glass. Ari tread carefully around it.

"I would like to exchange navigational skills. I could teach you to navigate the written word, and you could teach me to navigate the stars. At the most basic level, of course. I realize that I could never hope to achieve your level of piloting skill."

The glass slid away as Orin blinked slowly at him. His lips twitched before settling into a thoughtful frown. One long index finger came up to trace the edge of the open page with surprising delicacy. He leaned forward to hunch over the book, leaving Ari staring at the top of his head. His voice was soft but lined with gravel, all traces of arrogance abandoned.

"I won't be any good at it."

Ari sniffed dismissively, spinning the book around to face Orin properly.

"I shall be the judge of that."

*

The noise volume of the next establishment was nearly as overwhelming as the stench of the last one, the heavy beat of synth music battering Ari's ears before they had even entered the swinging doors.

He simply could not understand how anyone could enjoy themselves when one was unable to hear oneself think.

Orin wrapped his arm around Ari's waist, pulling him tight to his side as he led them through the writhing throng of bodies crowding the floor, all moving together in time to the pulsating rhythm hammering a dull ache in Ari's head.

An unfamiliar hand snaked around his waist from the other side, squeezing his hip as Orin shoved through the tightly packed couples ahead of them. Ari checked over his shoulder in fear, but no one was there.

It took several minutes before they finally broke through to the other side, the music still blaring but not quite as overwhelming as it had been on the dance floor.

Orin shouldered a visibly inebriated man aside to push Ari into the corner and pulled a chair over for him. Ari sat gingerly, trying not to touch the crusty metal arms with his hands. Orin grabbed onto them without a thought as he leaned in, lips moving against the shell of Ari's ear as he pressed in close enough to be heard.

"You don't let nobody bring you a drink, you don't take nothing the server didn't give you directly, you hear me?"

Ari nodded, throat closing against the thought of attempting to shout back over the music.

Orin squeezed his shoulder. "Good. Now you wait right here. I spotted our singer when we were walking in. I'll be back in two shakes."

Ari watched him dive back into the crowd, head visible above the dancers as he waded through without an ounce of hesitation.

Ari twisted his hands in his lap, fighting back the nonsensical feeling of missing him already. It was ridiculous. The man had practically spent all night and day beside him. All the same, Ari couldn't shake the feeling. He didn't want to be apart from Orin; he missed standing beside him, holding him, feeling him above and inside him. It was like an addiction.

Absolutely ridiculous, to crave such a connection at all times like this. Ari blanched at the sudden thought that he might be a natural-born, round-heeled slut, that having had a taste of it, he'd flop on his back for any man who asked him.

He scanned the room surreptitiously, picking out a few men among the strangers in the crowd who could be considered attractive. There, big and broad and corded with muscle, inoffensive face, even a few scars for interest. Or that one, handsome face and wide shoulders, long-fingered hand gripping his drink like a lifeline. Or even him, with wide blue eyes and hair like spun gold, hips gyrating to the music.

To his relief, Ari felt not the slightest inclination to bed any of these men.

Orin glanced over at him above the crowd with a little smile and, oh.

Perhaps he was just an extremely focused round-heeled slut.

Ari decided he could live with that.

His thoughts were interrupted by the blond man he'd had just been considering. The man leaned in far too closely, sweaty face brushing against Ari's jaw as he shouted in his ear.

"Can I buy you a drink?"

Ari backed away as far as he could, shaking his head vehemently.

The man slid onto the badly stained chair across from Ari, laying a hand on his arm as he continued to shout, "Well, then, why don't I just keep you company for a spell?"

Ari shouted his refusal over the music, but the man gave no indication of having heard him. He leaned in too close again, hand extended for Ari to shake.

"Name's Randy, nice to meet you."

As Ari reluctantly accepted the handshake, Randy's other hand slithered up the inside of Ari's thigh, stopping with a sickening squeeze inches from his crotch. Ari yelped as he cringed back with disgust, struggling to free his hand from Randy's grip, pushing the other hand away forcefully.

Randy's smile was sharp around the edges, white teeth gleaming in the multicolored lights bouncing off the dance floor. "Not from around here, are you?"

Ari declined to answer, contorting himself out of the boxed-in chair and shoving his way into the crowd in search of Orin.

Bodies knocked into him from every side, the scent of sweat and perfume thick in his throat. Strange hands touched and squeezed and pinched as Ari grew increasingly frantic, struggling across the floor.

He finally spotted Orin with a sigh of relief and made his way over until he could see him clearly. Ari stood frozen in shock as he watched Orin move together with a strange man on the dance floor.

The stranger was fine-boned and handsome, long elegant arms exposed by rolled-up sleeves as he wound them around Orin's neck. Ari couldn't help noticing the practiced movement of Orin's hands as they moved over the stranger's hips, pressing him close. Orin nuzzled his face into the stranger's neck, lips moving against his skin as Ari's heart dropped to the floor, pummeled beneath the dancing feet of everyone around him.

Orin lifted his head and caught sight of Ari, his whole body stilling for a moment before he looked back down at the stranger with a laugh, allowing him to move the hair out of his face with a caressing hand.

Ari was jolted into motion, moving resolutely toward the exit even as he was buffeted about by the dancers. Someone grabbed at his backside, but Ari just kept moving, wiping the sweat from his eyes with his sleeve.

It was a good deal of sweat.

The establishment was overheated, that was all.

Ari pushed out into the relatively fresh air with a stifled gasp and leaned against the dented wall. He took a few moments to gather himself before walking off in the direction of the docks, scrupulously avoiding brushing shoulders with the nighttime crowds spilling out into the settlement's streets.

Ari had reached the dock and was heading for his ship when he heard Orin calling. He tilted his head over his shoulder to see Orin approaching at a long-legged trot, sleeves rolled up and shirt unbuttoned to the waist. Ari turned back and increased his pace.

Orin caught up with him regardless, wiping his brow as he snagged Ari's shoulder. "Green looks good on you, Red."

Ari spun on his heel, prodding Orin's wide chest with one indignant finger, gaining ground as his companion backed up a step. "Envy. Green is representative of envy. You ignorant buffoon. Envy and jealousy are two entirely separate concepts. You are trying to imply that I am jealous. Which, I can assure you, I am not."

Orin nodded, stepping back another pace, arms hanging at his sides, chest still heaving with exertion.

Ari's fingers curled into fists, planted firmly on his narrow hips, arms akimbo.

"It would be ridiculous for me to be jealous! Whatever ill-advised nonsense you engage in during your spare time is none of my affair. Your excessive flirting and promiscuous behavior at every. Single. Port we dock in has absolutely no effect on me whatsoever! Just because we have engaged in some amorous activities does not mean that I have any right or inclination to object when you attempt to engage in those same activities with the first pox-eyed, rusted floozy you encounter!"

He was forced to pause for breath, surprised to find an unpleasant pressure in his chest which appeared to have nothing to do with running out of breath. His eyes pricked with tears, face flushed with heat. A rush of humiliation washed over him, leaving him shaking and exposed in the middle of the filthy dock.

Orin had lifted his head, surprise spreading across his face as Aristotle's voice continued to rise. The left corner of his lips threatened to lift, dimple winking in and out of view.

"You know I wasn't interested in getting that singer on his back. I was just coming on all friendly to try and figure out if he could give us coordinates for an exit point. And I got em, baby. We're all set to head out whenever you're ready."

Ari couldn't withstand his hopeful expression, all the bravado from his tirade deflating at once. He suddenly felt very small.

"Good. That's good. I— Thank you. I fear I owe you an apology. It shouldn't matter if you had been courting that singer anyway."

He ignored Orin's brows flying up as he mouthed *courting* in exaggerated disbelief.

"You are, of course, free to pursue a relationship, physical or otherwise, with whomever you wish. I apologize. I should not have reacted in such an inflammatory manner. It is perfectly understandable. I would not be surprised if my fumbling attentions have been insufficient to satisfy your needs. Who am I to quibble over your personal life? I am nothing to you beyond your temporary business partner. It is not— It is not as though we have ever had any sort of discussion negotiating exclusivity between us."

"Isn't that what we're having now?" Orin asked softly. "A discussion about exclusivity?"

He enunciated each word with exaggerated care, scanning Ari's face. Orin raised a hand to his mouth and chewed at the rough skin around his thumbnail with studied casualness as he focused somewhere past Aristotle's shoulder.

Ari found himself blinking in astonishment. "Well, I— Yes, I suppose that we are."

Orin nodded slowly, shoving both hands deep in his pockets as he shifted his weight, scuffing one heavy boot heel on the ground. "That something you'd want? With me, I mean?" He flicked his head to the side, throwing sweat-damp hair off his forehead as he watched Ari with a serious expression. "I know I've got nothing to offer you but a big dick and a pilot's license."

Ari took a step closer, hooking a finger in one thick belt loop with a shy smile. "I must confess to being inordinately fond of your pilot's license."

The answering grin on Orin's face grew so sweetly and slowly it was like pouring honey over ice.

Chapter Eighteen

"Nice ride, Stone."

Ari watched Orin's hackles rise as the morning quiet of the dock was disturbed by an unfamiliar and unpleasantly nasal voice. Orin set the supply crate down next to the ramp, dusted his hands off on his trousers, and turned to face the shabbily dressed trio of men approaching them across the dock.

"And the ship ain't too bad neither!" the tallest one continued, throwing his head back with a wheezing laugh before blowing a wet kiss in Ari's direction.

Ari edged back against the ship, bolstered by the solid metal behind him, trying to press hard enough to inject some steel in his spine.

Orin glanced over at him before lazily stepping closer to the men, blocking Ari from their sight. He hooked his hands in his braces, rocking back on his heels.

"Thought I might've smelled y'all coming. Mind standing downwind, Darryl? Do us all a favor."

The other two men guffawed, slapping their sour-faced companion on the back as he glared at Orin.

Ari started making his way toward the ramp, head down and trying his best to avoid everyone's attention.

The bearded man to Orin's left ogled Ari shamelessly, roving from his carefully parted hair to the laces of his boots before turning to Orin with a baffled expression.

"Hey, wasn't you walking out with a lady friend last I saw you? Didn't take you for the pretty-boy type."

Darryl's laugh had a dark edge of cruelty as he leered at Ari while mimicking Orin's stance with thumbs hooked in his own dirty canvas braces.

"Oh, you didn't know? Now see—Stone—he's anyone's dog who'll hunt. Don't care what they got in the engine room; he's in that cockpit quick as a whip. Ain't exactly what you'd call discriminating. It's all in his upbringing, if you ask me. Too much time around whores like his mother. Never got no proper schooling, but he sure learned how to drop his drawers for half a credit."

Ari turned to Orin and found traces of hurt visible through the cracks in his impassive mask. A shocking surge of violence rose in his gut, hands rolling into fists as he contemplated how satisfying it would be to disarrange Darryl's coarse features.

Orin's hands dropped to his hips, resting there in a relaxed stance, right middle finger absently tapping against the butt of his pistol.

"You know, Darryl, I think we'd all breathe a sight better if you'd just crawl back into whatever puddle of piss you rolled out of this morning."

The third man started inching away from his companions, bloodshot gray eyes fixed on Orin's tapping finger. Ari did the opposite, changing course to move closer to Orin, observing the rising tension beneath his casual swagger.

Darryl's face contorted in an ugly sneer, hands clenching around his braces.

"You owe us, Stone. That was our cargo got dumped when you surrendered your ship to Enforcers like a greenhorn on his first jump. You should've stayed in the dark with the raiders. Showing your rusted face round here, bold as brass? Well, seems to me that's gotta mean you're prepared to compensate us for our losses."

His face twitched to Ari and back to Orin, oily sneer oozing across like a grease stain.

"Could cut you a deal, if you're a few credits short, for old time's sake. Let us take your fancy new ride out for a spin. Looks like he'd be a screamer, and I like 'em loud."

Orin's gun was in his hand before Darryl could shut his mouth, his other arm sweeping around to push Ari behind him. Ari deeply regretted leaving his own firearm on the ship, noticing, with a sinking stomach, the heavily laden holsters of the men before them.

Darryl stepped closer, and the hair at the back of Ari's neck rose at the low buzz of Orin's pistol charging.

Darryl released his braces, holding his hands palm out at his shoulders. "Now, now, no call for violence. Your little robin red-breast is safe from us. Long as we get what's coming to us, mind." His smile was as thin and sharp as razor wire, eyes flicking from Orin's gun to his companions, who nodded before stepping away in either direction.

Orin flinched slightly at the movement, whole body growing still as every muscle tensed along his back.

Ari pushed past Orin, stopping short as Orin's hand clamped down like iron on his forearm. But Ari laid his own hand gently over Orin's fingers and addressed the men as a group. "I propose that we settle this like gentlemen."

The trio exchanged confused glances. Then Darryl turned to Ari and spit on the ground between them.

"Don't see no gentlemen around here. How 'bout you fellas?"

The bearded man pointed at Ari, then yelped when Darryl smacked his arm back down to his side.

Ari turned his head to catch Orin's attention. Barely moving his lips and keeping his voice too low to carry, he asked, "How much?"

Orin twisted away from Ari to glare at the men shifting impatiently on their feet as they watched the exchange.

He dropped the number like he was spitting out a seed. "Twenty."

Ari's brows lifted incredulously. "Just twenty credits?"

Orin shook his head slightly, lips dipping in a frown. "Thousand."

If Ari's eyebrows had been capable of levitation, this would have been the moment he discovered it.

"Twenty thousand credits!" His voice squeaked as he repeated the number a little louder than he meant to, earning a suspicious squint from Darryl. "Orin, that's. That is not an insignificant amount."

Orin shrugged, pulling Ari back slightly as he stepped forward, edging one of his enormous boots in front of Ari's feet.

"I know. Figured I'd take care of it after I got Delilah all squared away as a one-man kinda girl. Mighty hard for a pilot to line his pockets without a ship."

Darryl twitched his head, and his two companions started to move, circling around to either side of Orin's position in front of the ship.

Orin's hand tightened on Ari's arm, fingertips digging in harder than he probably intended. Ari squeezed his own hand over Orin's fingers, drawing a brief glance as Orin swiveled his head to keep sight of the men moving toward them.

"I'll pay it," Ari said.

Orin's fingers spasmed around his arm with enough force to cause Ari to wince, and he dropped his hand as soon as he saw his expression. "Can't let you do that. I'm not worth it, sweetheart. Ain't exactly a sound investment."

Ari was already shaking him off, drawing his pad out of his pocket with a determined stride. He wrinkled his nose at Darryl when he drew close enough to discover that Orin had not really been joking about the smell. Ari struggled to keep the disgust from his face, speaking as evenly as he could manage.

"Will you accept Ident or Chip?"

Darryl snatched the pad and pressed his fingers to the screen hard enough to leave thick smudges of grime behind. At the beep, he pulled away with a satisfied smirk. He leered at Ari before turning the full oily force of his personality on Orin.

"Sure hope you're going for more than half a credit these days, Stone. You'll be spending years on your back to pay this off. Gonna have to ask real nice for your fancyman to buy you some chafing cream."

Ari had a sudden and vivid daydream of smashing his fist into Darryl's snide mouth, feeling his teeth cut into his knuckles as they broke and bled, watching him spit the shattered pieces on the ground between them.

Instead, he turned on his heel and caught a glimpse of a stricken-faced Orin before heading off toward the open ramp. He skirted around the openly staring bearded man as they passed each other going in opposite directions.

Ari did some rapid calculations in his head. His and Theo's funds were not bottomless. In fact, Ari would find himself scraping the bottom if he did not locate Theo very soon.

It didn't matter. They could economize. Sell their possessions, move into more modest lodgings and procure salaried positions, perhaps. Less time for their academic pursuits, but Ari could live with that. As long as Theo was safe and Orin was finally able to call a ship his own. Ari could live with a lot of things if it kept a smile on both of those faces, he was discovering.

Ari turned back so quickly he nearly fell off the ramp, half ducking at the unmistakable sound of a laser pistol discharging behind him.

Darryl sat on the ground, face ashen as he stared at the wide scorch mark centimeters from his feet. The gray-eyed man took off down the docks at a sprint as the bearded man gave a long-suffering sigh and went to help Darryl to his feet.

Orin waved them off cheerfully, gun dangled casually from his thumb.

"Would you look at that? Faulty trigger, most like. Awful sorry about that, boys! Y'all have a pleasant afternoon, now!"

Orin waited until the men had walked out of sight before he turned around to give Ari a determined scowl, holstered his pistol, and headed toward the ramp.

Ari backed up a step, gesturing to the stack of crates waiting to be loaded. "I need you to finish preparations. We have spent long enough on this disgusting dock, and time is of the essence."

Something in Orin's face slammed shut as he nodded brusquely, changing course to haul a crate into the storage compartment.

Ari walked straight into the laboratory to sanitize his pad before pulling up Theo's notes with shaking hands.

*

Orin didn't turn his head when Ari entered the cockpit, but Ari could feel his attention on him just the same.

Something about the way the line of his shoulders rode a fraction higher and the slight tilt of his head, almost like he was listening intently for Ari's voice.

Ari didn't know what to say. What does one say to one's pilot and bed partner as one prepares to flout the law and jump the Verge in a desperate leap of faith?

Ari took a deep breath in through the nose, attempting to still the persistent tremor in his hands as he fastened his buckle. "Is everything in order?" He winced at the strident tone of his voice, an ugly sign of his unfortunate tendency to cling to formality in the face of uncertainty.

Orin gave a small grunt of affirmation, fingers flying over the incomprehensible numbers busily flooding his screen. He paused once a small green light blinked on the dash, indicating that coordinates had been entered successfully. Clearing his throat, he braced large hands on his knees as he swiveled to face Ari, jaw set.

"Didn't need you to do that. My debts are my own."

Ari was unsuccessful in repressing the shake in his hands, folding them together in his lap to hide them away. "I understand that you have your pride, but—"

Orin bared his teeth, hands clenching on his thighs. "Seems to me you don't understand. Seems to me you just dropped two bushels on a whim. I look like a helpless damsel to you?"

Ari shook his head, chewing hard on his lip.

Orin's expression softened at something in Ari's face, but his jaw stayed tense, hands still clenched.

"Didn't need saving. I can take care of myself just like I always done. I can't—I won't be beholden to you. Not like that. Understand? You'll get your credits soon as I'm able. And I won't be earning them through the family business like that piece of flotsam said. Ain't never gonna be like that between you and me."

Ari choked on air, horrified at the notion that Orin could even think he would ever consider using him in such a despicable manner.

"No. Of course not. You are my pilot and my—my friend. And you deserve nothing less than my respect. I would never ask such a thing of you; I can assure you. I did not assume your debt with the intention of requiring anything of you in return."

The fire dimmed in Orin, jaw relaxing slightly but hands still curled up tight.

Ari smoothed his own hands over his harness, gripping the strap across his hips as he continued. "However. In regards to the possibility of repayment, I...well... The truth is that there is a very good chance we shall never cross paths again after I find my brother. I have no manner of determining whether I will be able to find my way back through the dark after you and I have parted ways. If that is indeed the case, then I beg you to consider it a gift, from a friend who wishes you well. I find that I cannot bear the thought of you being forced to live on the run from such deplorable scoundrels and ruffians when I could have prevented it."

Orin's fingers unclenched to drift idly over the controls as he swiveled to face the view screen. "Like I said, you'll get your credits soon as I'm able. Never know, maybe I'll find you when you cross back over the Verge. Buy you a drink back in that saloon where we first met.

The one that had you twitching like you was itching for a bath just from touching the door. Walking in pretty as a picture in your fancy clothes like you never had dirt under your fingernails in all your life. I swear, I never seen a head of hair I wanted to ruffle more."

Orin's dimples made a full appearance as he flashed his charming smile, something so melancholy hiding in his face Ari had to look away, swallowing against a lump in his throat.

"Yes, I suppose that would be a very favorable outcome, indeed. I would be pleased to meet you on this side of the Verge, if I am ever afforded the opportunity to do so."

Orin's eyes crinkled at the corners as he stole another glance at Ari before returning to his numbers.

Ari continued, voice barely held above a whisper, prodded by a twisting pain in his chest. "Do you know, when I first saw you waiting there in that filthy saloon, I nearly turned tail and gave it all up for a bad job? You were so big and...and so very handsome and worldly and just everything I thought I could never have, right there in front of me. It required every ounce of my courage just to sit at your table, much less ask for your help. I believe I will live the rest of my life grateful for that moment of courage and all it has brought to me, grateful for your assistance and your companionship."

They shared a precious selection of silent moments, each one falling between them like a handful of diamonds slipping from Ari's shaking fingers onto the metal floor.

Ari was the first to break away, nodding once decisively as he faced the shimmering wall of the Verge through the view screen. He had never been so close. Those born on the interior ring of Core worlds rarely got a chance to venture beyond the colonies lining the barrier.

"Well, time to dip into that courage once again. Nothing for it now but to press forward. Just think, soon you will be approaching the barrier of the Verge from the other side in your very own ship. And I, should the stars choose to shine, will have my brother safe within my arms. Everything we ever wanted, the both of us, could be just on the other side of this jump."

Orin summoned up another smile, but this one blurred around the edges, water gathering across Ari's vision at an unsuitable rate for such a happy occasion.

"I got Delilah fixed on the exit point," Orin said, "ready to jump when you are, professor."

Ari observed with frayed nerves as Orin steered them toward the swirling translucent veil of the Verge at a reasonable speed, neither fast nor slow enough to be particularly noticeable to any passing ships.

Ari stiffened his posture as Orin checked over his numbers, thick fingers moving across the flight controls steadily.

He studied Orin's face, resolutely turned toward the view screen, brow furrowed with concentration.

Ari took a deep breath as he beheld the interior wall of the enormous force field, the glimmering brightness nearly blinding as they drew closer and closer. "Is that—is that it? You just enter the right numbers and we can get through?"

Orin quirked his lips to the side, glancing at Ari briefly before checking his numbers again. "Told you, sweetheart. You get your numbers right and you can go anywhere. Even beyond the Verge."

Ari gripped his armrests tightly as the barrier of the Verge loomed bright and huge and distressingly solid before them.

Tilting his head toward Ari, Orin practically vibrated with excitement as his hands gripped the flight controls. "You ready for this?"

Ari nodded, swallowing his fear as he closed his eyes and thought of Theo's beloved laugh, the unattractive snorting sound he made when something was so irresistibly amusing that he lost all control. That humble sound bolstered Ari's courage beyond what he ever thought possible.

"Yes. Let's do it," he said.

Orin whooped as the ship suddenly dropped and turned, dorsal fin skimming along the Verge with a harsh electric buzz that set Ari's teeth on edge until, suddenly, they were through.

Ari opened his eyes to stare at the shimmering swirl of the external dome, nothing but the expanse of the deep dark at their back.

"That's my girl, Delilah! Yes, ma'am!" Orin cheered and patted the dash as Ari wrapped his arms around himself in an attempt to contain the full-body shudder at the overwhelming expanse of the dark pressing in from all sides.

Orin quieted down, and Ari turned to features tight with concern.

"You alright, sweetheart?"

Ari nodded, straightening his posture as he dropped his hands into his lap. "Yes. You did an exemplary job. I could not have asked for a better pilot."

"Not much further to go now." Orin reached out to Ari and squeezed his hand gently. "Just a little trip through the deep dark to get to the Restricted Sector, maybe a few days more at the outside. Let's go fetch your boy."

Ari squeezed back gratefully before Orin returned to the controls, where the pilot turned the ship away from the exterior wall of the Verge and increased their speed, the dark closing in around them.

Chapter Nineteen

Forty-eight hours. Two full cycles in the dark, poring over every clue at Ari's disposal until it felt like the walls of his laboratory were closing in around him.

Tantalum. Tattoos. Hangul.

Strung together, they wove a pathetically open net with which to catch his brother, the holes between each meager piece of information so large Orin could have steered Delilah right through them.

To make matters worse, Ari had awoken that morning to an empty bunk, Orin having crammed himself back into the maintenance hatch to repair some malfunction in the accelerator which, for now, kept them plodding through the dark at an excruciating pace.

Today was not the day Ari wished to spend on anxious contemplation of all the information he didn't have and all the myriad ways things could go wrong.

Today of all days, he should be thinking only of his brother, but instead, he yearned for some distraction from his spiraling anxiety.

He popped up from where he had been resting dejectedly against his workbench at the sound of the maintenance hatch slamming shut, hinges squealing in protest.

Ari peeked out of his lab at Orin standing in the corridor clad in nothing but trousers, skin shining with perspiration and streaks of machine oil as he attempted to clean his hands with a threadbare rag. His shirt lay in a disorderly pile at his feet, the cream linen thankfully free of grease as far as Ari could tell.

He must have made some sound for Orin to lift his head so suddenly, zeroing in one Ari, something black smudged from his forehead to the crest of his left cheekbone.

"Think I found the problem," he said. "Good news is I can fix it. Bad news is it's gonna take me a minute."

Ari stepped into the corridor, picked up Orin's shirt, and shook it out for a cursory inspection before folding it neatly into thirds. He watched Orin scrub the rag over his arms, spreading the grease more than he was removing it.

"Approximately how long is a minute in this scenario?" Ari asked.

Orin twisted and crumpled the rag between his hands, face apologetic. "Maybe two more days. I'm sorry, I know you're itching to get there."

Guilt stabbed at Ari with the strength of a hundred flaming swords as he realized he was actually somewhat relieved by the delay, dreading the moment Orin would fly away into the dark almost as much as he was anxious to make progress in his search for Theo.

Orin stretched as far as he was able in the corridor, back flexing as he worked out the kinks from being crammed into the hatch. Ari's stomach clenched at the sight, knees aching to drop in front of Orin so he could open those trousers with his teeth. Yearning for distraction, indeed.

Ari was a terrible brother.

He shifted on his feet, holding his bundle of linen low enough over his own trousers to have a hope of subtlety. "Will you be occupied with repairs for the remainder of the day cycle?" he asked, voice cracking in a mortifying fashion.

Orin paused his ineffectual scrubbing, attention dropping to his shirt in Ari's hands and up to Ari's face, dimples flashing like a wink.

"Naw, she's gonna need a few hours just chugging along like this before I can get in there again and expect to get anything done. I gotta jump in the sonic for now; think there's not an inch of me left clean."

Ari nodded distractedly, following the rippling muscles in Orin's back as he turned and walked into his bunk, door hissing shut behind him. Ari leaned against the metal paneling, eyes closed as he tried to burn the sight into his memory.

They flew open again at another hiss, at Orin standing square inside the doorway with his hands busily unbuttoning his trousers.

Orin tilted his head at Ari, one brow lifting inquisitively. "What you waiting out there for? C'mon in, beautiful."

He turned, stepped out of his trousers, and sauntered into the en suite without a single care for his nudity, leaving both doors open behind him.

Ari sat on the rumpled sheets of Orin's bunk to wait as the sonic thrummed along, efficiently cleaning all traces of grease from Orin's skin. He folded and refolded Orin's clothing, every corner perfectly neat by the time Ari laid them on the desk.

He was presumptive enough to remove his own boots and waistcoat, lining them up next to the stack of folded clothes.

Even though he was waiting for it, Ari still jumped at the sound of the sonic shutting off, head snapping to the open doorway.

Orin stepped through with an easy swagger, gaze skimming over Ari and sending warmth against his skin. "Why you still got all your clothes on?"

Orin knelt on the floor to work Ari's trousers open as Ari pulled his shirt over his head, the shirt ending up folded atop his waistcoat and the trousers tossed in a heap to the side.

Ari scooted back until his head hit the pillow as Orin crawled up the bed like a stalking cat, the day-cycle lighting in his bunk bouncing off his coiled muscles as though he were still covered in oil. Ari swallowed thickly at the sight.

Orin knelt between Ari's knees and dragged a hand over Ari's chest.

"Oughta keep you like this, spread out in my bed naked as the day you were born. Well, except for these. You can leave these right where they are, sugar."

He toyed with the small bow of Ari's garter just above his right knee. Ari tangled their fingers as he tried to work the knot free, but Orin brought their clasped hands up to his lips with a gentle kiss, searching Ari's face.

"Would you mind leaving them? Just the once?"

Ari shivered at the delicious flash of hunger in Orin's eyes. He shrugged self-consciously, turning away to focus on the wall beside them.

"They're only stockings, everyone wears them back home. Mine aren't even particularly decorative. Just simple white silk knit and plain black ribbon. Hardly worth your notice, I'm afraid."

Orin's hands smoothed down Ari's stockings, the callouses on his palms catching at the delicate material, his bottom lip clamped between his teeth.

"Honey, if you could see yourself. Legs for miles, all tied up with a pretty little bow. My best dreams aren't half as good as this, gorgeous."

Heat rushed to Ari's face at a fraction of the rate that it rushed to his cock under the rough tone of Orin's voice. Ari straightened the seams on his stockings, nervous fingers centering the bows. Orin's gaze followed his hands, dark with desire.

Ari smoothed the top edge once more, then dropped his hands to rest on the tensed muscles of Orin's forearms bracketing his hips on the bed. "I suppose that would be acceptable. Provided we do not ruin them, for I haven't an inexhaustible supply aboard the ship."

Orin traced the bows with whisper-soft fingers, barely disturbing the fabric at all. "I'll be real careful. Promise."

Ari fidgeted in place, feeling particularly ridiculous and exposed despite the fact that he was wearing the most clothing.

Orin didn't seem to notice, every ounce of his focus dedicated to the length of Ari's legs, the weight of his eyes heavier than the delicate touch of his fingertips on the bows.

Ari lifted onto an elbow and wrapped his other hand behind Orin's neck, finally gaining his attention as he brought him down for a kiss. He licked and nipped at his lips until Orin pushed deeper with a groan, tongue swiping at the roof of his mouth.

Ari shivered, bowing his back to press their chests together. Orin's arm came around to support his weight, pulling him up onto Orin's thighs. Ari straddled his hips as Orin sat up against the wall.

Ari clutched at Orin's shoulders, head thrown back with a cry as Orin's head dipped to pull a nipple into his mouth, sucking hard enough to leave a red mark on Ari's chest.

"So pretty. Just look at you. You like that?"

Ari didn't answer so much as push his chest into Orin's face as he gave the same attention to his other nipple with a low laugh that vibrated across his skin.

He fisted his hand in Orin's hair as he bit and licked across Ari's chest.

Orin dipped his hands to cup and squeeze Ari's ass, then spread him open and ran light fingers over his hole. "You want me, baby? Like that?"

Ari tugged his head up to smear their lips together, wrapping his legs tightly around Orin's waist.

"Yes. Just like that. Please."

Orin made a low noise in his throat as he toppled Ari onto the bed, one hand suddenly gripping the bottle of lubricant, fingers already slick.

Ari lifted his hips off the bed as Orin's hand slid between his legs, fingers swirling firmly on the patch of skin behind his testicles before easing slowly into him one at a time, working him open gently but thoroughly.

Ari rested a hand on Orin's wrist, mouth dropping open as Orin honed in on that spot, rubbing maddening little circles that coursed like lightning up Ari's spine. His voice grew thready and thin as if he couldn't get enough air. A secret part of him felt like he didn't need air when he had Orin like this.

"Good. That's good. I'm ready now."

Orin gave a thoughtful hum, fingers twisting and stretching, his wrist flexing under Ari's fingertips. "Almost there, gorgeous. Stars, you're still so tight around me."

He grunted as Ari clenched around his fingers, then pulled them out almost too quickly as he dropped onto his elbows over Ari's head and pushed the burning length of his cock into the damp crease of Ari's thigh.

Ari whined, dipped his hand between them to wrap around his own cock with a squeeze in a thoughtless attempt to relieve some of the pressure. He let go with a hot rush of shame as soon as he noticed Orin observing him closely. So he drew his hands up beside his head, curling the guilty one into a tight fist as he closed his eyes, skin burning with a prickling flush all the way down to his chest.

"Sorry. I know I oughtn't. I'm sorry."

Orin leaned onto one elbow, startling him, and uncurled Ari's fist to press a gentle kiss into his palm. "Nothing to be sorry for. I love watching you touch yourself, gorgeous."

Ari slitted his lids open to catch a glimpse of Orin's patient face. "You don't think it's— That I'm—you know, shameful? For that?"

Orin shook his head slowly, eyes clutched so tightly to Ari's he couldn't look away despite the tugging weight of his humiliation. "Sure don't. Never seen something so beautiful in all my life as your pretty little hands on your perfect body, sweetheart. Could stand to see some more of that, if you're willing to oblige."

The heat in Ari's face kept on burning, radiating over every inch of his body in a sweet ache at the throb of Orin's low voice. Ari dropped his arm to his side in an awkward, unsteady motion, hovering his hand over the flat plane of his stomach, searching Orin's face as he lowered the tips of his fingers to slide across his skin.

"You mean, like this?"

The sound that erupted from Orin's throat sent Ari's cock throbbing and twitching with a wet slap against his stomach just inches from his fingertips. Ari squeaked in mortification, but Orin's eyes darkened as he was forced to clear the growl from his throat before he could speak.

"That's perfect. Just like that, baby. Fuck, you're pretty."

Ari let the sweet words pour over him like a soothing balm, easing the prickling burn of his flush and the sting of his shame until he could wrap his hand around his cock once more, this time studying Orin as he followed Ari's hand, tongue flashing out to moisten his lips.

A surge of power burned away the last traces of Ari's shame, and he pumped his hand slowly as Orin tracked every movement, one of his own hands falling between them to squeeze tightly around the base of his cock.

Ari clenched around nothing at the sight, and he dropped his hands to flail madly around the bedding in search of the bottle. Half sitting up, he opened it with clumsy fingers, spilling a few drops onto his stomach before pooling some into his hand.

He quickly spread it over Orin's cock, using so much in his exuberance that it dripped onto the bed between them.

Orin took the bottle from him and made it disappear into the sheets once more. As he sat up on his knees, Orin guided Ari's hand to slick his own cock as Orin pressed against him with intent.

Ari panted through his entry, raising his feet to rest on Orin's hips as he gave a strangled shout once Orin finally bottomed out.

Orin lifted Ari's legs onto his shoulders, pressing a kiss to his ankle as he slid them past his neck, the soft silk of the stockings barely catching at the hair on his chest. He then started a careful rhythm, focused on Ari's face as he moved his hips, hands restlessly running up and down Ari's legs like he wasn't quite aware he was doing it.

Ari cried out as Orin leaned forward, burying his fists into the bed beside Ari's ribs as his cock dragged across every bright spot inside him at once. He clutched at Orin's arms, fingertips digging in.

"Oh, there! There, just there. Please, Orin."

Orin's mouth hung open, sweat starting to curl the fringe of his hair against his face and neck. He eased into slow, hard, deep thrusts, rubbing Ari perfectly with the thick length of his cock until Ari was a writhing mess beneath him.

Orin dropped onto his elbows as he stared down between their bodies at Ari's weeping cock, bobbing along with their movements.

"Can you touch yourself for me, baby? I want to see you come on my cock, and I'm so close already, honey. I'm sorry; you just feel so good like this."

Ari hushed him gently, pressing a kiss against the underside of his jaw as he obediently wrapped his hand around his cock, sliding easily along his silken skin.

Pushing up onto his fists with a low moan, Orin divided his attention between Ari's face and cock.

"There you are. Like that, gorgeous. Stars, look at you, you're so good like this. I could watch you all damn day."

Ari cried out sharply as he pulsed in his hand, spilling over his chest and stomach as he clenched around Orin's pumping length.

Orin lowered Ari's legs to the side and slid his hands under Ari's back in a tight embrace as they kissed with open mouths, swapping panting breaths with every thrust.

Picking up speed, Orin pressed his face into Ari's hair with a choked groan as he spilled inside him in a throbbing burst of heat.

He eased out gently, kissing Ari's throat at the whine he couldn't prevent in protest of the loss, and flopped onto his back with a gusty sigh.

Ari melted into the bed at his side, shocking the both of them by bursting into tears.

Orin shot up immediately, hands hovering over the curled-up sobbing mess beside him as Ari tried to turn away.

"Sweetheart! What's wrong? Was I too rough with you?"

"N-no. No, of course not. N-nothing like that. You were—you were wonderful... I'm f-fine, it's nothing." Ari did his best to curtail the hitching of his chest, breathing deeply through his nose as he dashed at his cheeks with sticky fists.

Orin tugged on his shoulder until he fell to his back. As Ari stared up at the faintly glowing ceiling panels, Orin's hand ghosted over his chest and stomach with the sheet, cleaning him off before petting him softly. "Don't look fine to me. I gotta say, I've gotten some poor reviews before, but nobody's ever cried on me. What is it?"

Ari shook his head, rubbing the heels of his hands hard against his face. "It's truly nothing of consequence. It's foolish. I'm being ridiculous. I'm so sorry. This really isn't appropriate. I'm trying to stop."

Orin hummed into his neck, leaving a trail of kisses across his shoulder. "You could never be foolish, honey. Please tell me what it is."

"It's my birthday," Ari said beneath his breath, voice shaking despite his best efforts to calm himself.

Orin's face cleared into a gentle smile as he laid a smacking kiss on the crest of Ari's shoulder. "Happy birthday, gorgeous!"

Ari didn't react, twisting his fingers in the sheets at his hips as he struggled to breathe calmly and quietly.

Orin pushed up on his elbow. "You want to do something? If I'd'a known, I'd have a gift for you, but I don't. I'm sorry, sweetheart."

Something eased in Ari's chest at the sight of his handsome face scrunched up with concern. He ran his hands over Orin's shoulders in reassurance.

"It isn't that. I would never expect you to present me with a gift. It's just. I've never had a birthday on my own before. It's our birthday, mine and Theo's. And I just— I miss him, today. Fiercely. That's all it is. I'm terribly sorry for crying on you like that over something so trivial."

Orin laid back down, working his arm under Ari's head until he rested on the meat of his shoulder. Ari turned on his side to place one hand on Orin's chest, and Orin lay his cheek on top of Ari's head, stubble catching in his hair.

"Aw, baby. I'm sorry."

Ari took a few deep breaths, concentrating on the rough glide of Orin's fingertips up and down his arm. He hooked his leg over Orin's knee, the garter loose and the stocking pooled around his ankle.

"When is yours?" he asked quietly.

Now it was Orin's turn to stare at the ceiling.

"My what?"

Ari pushed up, baffled by his avoidance. "When is your birthday?"

Orin glanced at him and then back to the ceiling, moving the both of them with a deep shrug.

"Don't have one."

Ari gave a quiet laugh, searching for the joke. "Of course, you do. Everyone has a birthday!"

Orin pressed his lips into a tight line, hands moving restlessly over Ari's back.

"Not me."

"How do you know how old you are?"

Orin closed his eyes, hands falling away to land on the bed.

"Guess I don't. Not exactly."

Ari didn't know what to say, mouth working as he searched for words. All that escaped was a surprised gasp as Orin flipped them over, hovering over Ari on his hands and knees.

"Don't worry, sweetheart, I'm plenty old enough to take good care of you."

He smirked as he dropped to mouth at Ari's chest, pulling a still-red nipple gently between his teeth. Ari gasped again, tempted to go another round but instead, pushed at Orin's shoulders until he popped off.

Ari offered a small smile, stomach fluttering with nerves. "It's today."

Orin nodded, mouth rising into a smirk. "Yeah, I know, baby. It's your birthday. Gonna—"

"And. And. And yours," Ari pushed out quietly.

Orin shook his head, smirk fading in confusion as his hair flopped down over his forehead. "What?"

Ari lifted a hand to Orin's cheek, just holding him as they gazed at each other, and reached with his other hand to close over Orin's on the bed.

"It could be yours as well. If you—if you want it. You can share with me, with us. Me and Theo. You would be doing me a favor, truly. I would be ever so grateful if you would accept today as your birthday. That is, if you don't mind sharing. I'm sorry. It's stupid. Forget I ever—"

"Baby."

Orin's eyes were wide and stricken, growing red around the edges as they stayed glued to Ari's. They'd been nude in bed for over an hour now, but for the first time, Orin seemed truly naked.

"You would do that for me?"

Ari nodded, running his fingers through Orin's hair, curling gently around his ear as he rubbed his thumb over the soft curve of his earlobe.

"Of course."

Orin nudged against his hand, nuzzling into his palm, long lashes fluttering damp against his skin.

"Thank you, Ari."

Ari pressed their lips together over and over again, soft, tender, chaste kisses belying the fact that they were still lying in ruined sheets.

He dropped his head to Orin's chest to catch his breath. Orin's heart thumped strong and sure beneath his ear, cheek pillowed against his broad pectoral muscle, nose tickled by the curling hairs sprinkled across.

Ari sank into the embrace, mouth moving before he could think better of it. "You must know by now that I—that I hold you in the highest regard."

One large hand smoothed along the length of his arm, tangling their fingers together as Orin huffed out a short breath, the barest indication of laughter.

He raised their joined hands to his face and brushed his lips across Ari's knuckles as their eyes met.

"I regard you too, professor."

Chapter Twenty

See now, this one is tricky. Just about the same backward as forward, and Orin never could tell the difference. Kinda like that other one that was the same upside down as right side up.

Orin bit the inside of his cheek in concentration as he painstakingly dragged the pen down the parchment at an angle he hoped was correct.

Probably didn't matter even if it wasn't. Aristotle was so smart. More than half of him was brains by weight and every bit of him was beautiful. He'd be able to figure it out, despite Orin's clumsy spelling and coarsely scrawled letters.

Not like Orin had much better to offer anyway.

He'd tried, for a little while, to copy out the interconnected swirls of proper script writing like Ari had tried to teach him, fooling with being a Core-born, educated man. All came to nothing, in the end. Just a mangled mess of botched lines and ink spots where there should be spaces.

Wasn't a soul around that could've interpreted that mess.

So, block letters it was, lines scratched out thick and uneven despite the care Orin was putting into every one.

Couldn't get his spacing right either. Letters all crowded on top of one another like ants in a flood and words too far apart. He'd tried putting a finger down between the end of one word and the start of the next like the schoolmistress had taught him those few years he got to sit in on classes, but his fingers were so much thicker now that it didn't look right anymore.

Looked exactly like what it was, which is to say, pathetic. Uglier than homemade sin.

He blew out a frustrated breath, grabbing at the sheets of parchment as they tried to fly off the desk in every direction.

Nothing had ever seized his chest quite like the sight he'd walked in on that morning, Ari bent over a pristine leather satchel, efficiently packing it to the brim with all manner of things.

Orin couldn't even appreciate the view properly, feeling like the wind had been knocked right out of him and aching from it.

Seeing that, just knowing that Ari was calmly preparing for their separation had sent pain all over like little cracks spiderwebbing through Orin's bones.

Mighty silly of him, coming down with the vapors over one measly little satchel.

Over one brilliant little redhead.

Deal's a deal, though, and that was the deal. All Orin had to do was set Ari down on the surface, and then he could take off in his very own ship.

Should sound like heaven, that.

Curious how it felt so much like torture.

Made sense, of course. Delilah wasn't built for a three-man crew anyhow. Just the two bunks to be had and only two seats bolted in the cockpit.

Sure, it might've crossed Orin's mind a time or two that maybe he could stow away in Ari's bunk, tuck his boots in next to Ari's every night like they'd gotten in the habit of doing lately.

But truth was, Ari probably wouldn't want his brother to know he'd been letting a brute like Orin warm his sheets. Couldn't blame him; it was clear as day Orin wasn't suited for a man like that. All silk underthings and ten-credit words.

He remembered the way Ari had said "courting" like it was something he expected Orin to be capable of. And maybe that had set him to thinking of all the ways Ari deserved to be courted, all the ways he probably would be once he made his way home.

Some fancy university man bringing him flowers and sweets and taking him out to museums and shows, strolling down the street arm in arm as proud as you please. Laying him down on satin sheets and kissing every single inch of that creamy skin at least twice every night.

And maybe Orin had wasted some time thinking about what it might be like if he could've been one of those men. If he had an education and a home and more than a busted-up toolbox and fifty credits to his name.

Once he got the ship repaired, though, there wouldn't be much time left for him to waste on contemplating impossible dreams. He'd get Ari to where he was going, and if he was lucky, he'd get to stick around long enough to see the joy on his face when he found his brother before Orin finally got the boot.

If Orin was a better man, he'd back out of the deal entirely. Refuse the ship and insist that Ari and Theo take it back home for themselves. They belonged back in the Core, insulated from the rough edges of space. Maybe Orin should stay behind in the Restricted Sector and barter his way home on his own or try to make his way as a pilot over there.

Might end up doing that anyway. Orin didn't have the faintest idea how he was just going to turn tail and head out when he knew Ari wasn't safe. No idea how he could leave him behind in the wilderness like that.

Every minute it seemed more and more likely Orin would end up breaking the deal and talking himself out of a ship for Ari's own good. Not even the lure of finally having his own ship again was enough to settle the rolling of his gut at the thought of leaving him alone in the Restricted Sector, far outside the protection of the Verge.

Time enough to make that decision when it came down to it. Not much use in dithering over it now.

Best to focus on the task at hand. He stabilized his wrist with the opposite hand and attempted to line up a squiggly one behind two of the pointy ones, overlapping lines a little no matter how hard he tried not to.

Damn. Flying upside down and backward in a rusted blindfold was easier than this.

Orin cursed every star in the dark as he splotched another ink blot on top of his words, dropping the pen with his big, clumsy fingers.

He leaned his head back, the little chair squeaking as he shifted his weight.

Tried thinking of nice things to calm him down. Things like gliding smooth through space with a powerful engine, or sitting down to a table laid out with all kinds of food, or putting his hand out and clasping another, smaller hand. Having that person look up at him with big green eyes and smiling pretty.

Visions of green eyes and sweet smiles sent him back to work, picking up the pen with a sigh and getting down to it.

*

Orin shifted the rolls of parchment under his arm as he clomped down the corridor, pausing when he found the cockpit unexpectedly occupied.

Ari sat in the pilot's chair, bent over and tapping away at the screen Orin usually used, ankles crossed primly beneath his seat.

"Whatcha doing there, sugar? Practicing those flight exercises I taught you?"

Ari whipped around like he'd been caught doing something he shouldn't, a dull flush rising up his neck.

"Oh, no. I'm sorry; I should practice those more often. I was just. Well. I suppose that I ought to go ahead and tell you. We may not have time later to go over everything in much detail."

Orin had a sinking feeling in his gut at the way Ari was coming across nervous as all get out. What did he have to say that he thought Orin wouldn't like?

Orin stepped closer to peek over Ari's shoulder as he turned back to the pilot's screen and continued tapping busily away.

"I was programming the coordinates of my lodgings on Britannia into the ship's navigational memory. I have also provided the entry code for the front and back doors. I would appreciate it if you could unload my and Theo's belongings there before being on your way. Of course, you are also welcome to stay there for as long as you wish. I cannot be certain when or if I shall return, and the lease has been paid for the remainder of the year."

Orin blinked hard against the sudden burning pressure of threatening tears. "You'd let a dirty Verge rat like me stay in your fancy digs?"

Ari spun around to face him, just about the picture of sincerity. "Of course, I would. And I forbid you to refer to yourself as such in future."

Orin rubbed the back of his hand under his nose with a loud sniff. "Mighty kind of you. How do you know I ain't gonna rob you blind?"

Ari considered Orin's chest, fingers running down the length of Orin's braces.

"I suppose I shall have to rely on trust in your good nature. Besides, you'll already be leaving with my most valuable possession, which I have given you freely."

Orin felt like he'd been dealt a punch to the gut as Ari lifted shining eyes to his, a tiny smile playing at his pretty lips. Orin wrinkled his nose, trying to clear his head after it went all funny at the sight.

"You mean Delilah?"

Ari's gaze dropped faster than a freighter with engine failure. "Yes, of course. The ship. I wish you well with it; I know it means a lot to you."

His hands trailed across Orin's chest and away, and then he stepped past Orin and out of the cockpit, face never lifting from the floor.

Orin felt like he was trying to lead them in a dance where he'd never learned any of the steps, just stumbling his bulk all over the floor and treading on Ari's toes.

He focused on the screen, accessing the memory logs and pulling up the set of numbers that were the key to Ari's house. Sweet thing had just handed it to him, like that wasn't the worst decision a fella could make. Inviting Orin to stay as long as he pleased, without a second thought.

Orin had never met anybody half as clever or naive. Dr. Aristotle Campbell was terrifying, honest truth.

Before he closed up the log, he added another level of security to the information in a surge of habitual caution. Locking up twice had got him this far, after all.

He adjusted the parchment, rolling it up tight and holding it in his hands as he walked back down the corridor. He could see into the open door of Ari's lab, Ari's back turned to him as he stood at his workbench, peering into some contraption or other and jotting down notes as easy as you please.

Wasn't even paying any attention to the paper, half the time.

Orin pulled up short behind him, not wanting to disturb his work. The parchment crumpled a little in his hand, the crunching sound bringing Ari's head up and around.

Those funny little goggles were shoved on his head again, mussing up his hair something fierce. Ari was completely ridiculous, brows raised inquisitively under the mess of red hair with the goggles perched on top like a crown.

Orin kind of loved them.

He shoved the roll of parchment out between them. "Here, take these and stash 'em somewhere safe, with whatever else you're packing for when we make landfall."

Ari furrowed his brow in confusion, goggles shifting precariously as he unrolled the first parchment. "What are they?"

Rubbing his hand over the back of his neck, Orin studied the workbench as if those neatly labeled rocks meant rust-all to him. "I charted as much as I know of the deep dark, plotted all the Verge entry points I could scrape together. Got a couple of places you can punch back through the barrier. Outlined my exit route from the

Restricted Sector for you. Made it real simple; any pilot worth his salt should be able to follow it out. Thought I'd leave you with a ticket home, if I could."

Ari lifted his gaze from the parchment, eyes huge and clear and so damn beautiful it hurt to look at them. Like taking a hard right hook to the chest, but twice as deep.

Orin had to take a deep breath to get through the phantom pain. "I know it's not much, and it sure as mud ain't perfect, but it'll getcha home if you get a half-decent pilot."

Ari sniffed at that, lip trembling, staring down at the parchment like it wasn't the saddest ink-blotted mess of scratches he'd ever seen. Like it was something worthwhile.

Orin shoved his hands in his pockets, shuffling his feet restlessly as Ari just continued to stare down at the parchment.

Something like shame clogged up his throat as he caught a glimpse over Ari's head at the mess on the paper. Something hot and sharp and crawling all over.

"Had to write out what I could in standard block." Orin's voice came out too loud as he tried not to dwell on it, bouncing off the metal cabinets in the laboratory. "Didn't know how to spell some of it, so you're gonna have to use that big brain to put it together. I know it's rough, but—"

Ari's lanky arms wrapped around him, squeezing tight enough that his ribs compressed, and the parchment dropped haphazardly on the table and rolled until it hit up against one of those rocks.

Orin pulled his hands out of his pockets and echoed the embrace, yanking Ari off his feet by accident.

Ari just laughed, hooking his legs up around Orin's hips as he climbed up to loop his arms over his shoulders, and Orin's hands curled automatically under his thighs.

Ari slid one of his hands from Orin's shoulder to curve over the nape of his neck. "Thank you."

His voice was so soft and sweet it wrapped around Orin's throat like a hand-knit scarf, soothing away that ache of shame he was still trying to swallow down.

Ari smiled up at him just like he did in his dreams, and Orin couldn't control the way his lips pressed softly to Ari's any more than he could control the stars.

Ari kissed him back harder and fiercer, hands gripping Orin's neck and shoulder tight.

Orin started walking until Ari's back pressed up against the wall, thighs tightening around his waist.

Those little brass goggles fell in a clattering mess to the floor at their feet.

Chapter Twenty-One

The ship ground to an absolute halt, the stillness heavy with bad portent, not even a single shudder of the engines running underfoot, just before the alarms started blaring.

The complete lack of motion sent nausea pooling in Ari's stomach faster than rocking loops and swift turns ever did. Orin worked silently, nostrils flaring as he ripped a panel from the dash to pick through the nest of wires underneath. He held his breath as he ripped some of them apart and twisted them back together again in a small shower of sparks, not even flinching when they landed against his skin.

Ari sat in the copilot's chair, lacing up his boots as lights flashed all around them. Orin remained barefoot but had thrown on a shirt, left hanging open with tails trailing down his hips as he squatted beneath the dash to tear open another panel.

Ari stared at the com light, the only dark spot on the wildly flashing dash.

"Do you think it is the Enforcers again?" he asked, trying to keep his voice level as he swallowed against the growing sense of dread.

Orin grunted, dropping a panel to the floor with an echoing *clang*.

"No Enforcers out here."

He cursed loudly under another shower of sparks, lights continuing to flash, but the alarms finally silenced in a void of sound so abrupt that it hurt, clapping against Ari's ears.

Orin popped open a small hatch and retrieved both of their weapons. Face stark, he handed Ari his pistol, igniting Ari's fear. "You remember everything I taught you. Always shoot first and aim true. Won't get a second chance out here."

Ari gripped his pistol with numb fingers, standing to follow Orin as he stalked out of the cockpit. Orin stopped him with a firm hand against his chest.

"You stay in there. I'm locking the doors behind me. It's the most defensible room in the ship. They'll come through the bay doors, but I'm gonna try to kick her engines back on before they can get in. Get ready to set Delilah going full throttle as soon as you're able."

Ari studied Orin's face, drawn tight and stark with a fear Ari had never seen there before. There was still a small mark in the shape of Ari's mouth peeking out of his collar, framed perfectly by the open halves of his rumpled shirt.

"What is happening? Who is coming? I don't understand."

Orin grabbed the back of Ari's head and pressed a hard kiss to his temple before stepping back over the threshold into the galley.

"Raiders," he said, hushed voice amplified in the sucking abyss of sound. "Now you get ready to be the pilot, honey. I'm giving her one last kick in the pants."

Ari shook his head, slapping his hand over the door panel before Orin could shut it. "I can't. I'm not— My brother is the brave one. Not me. Theo leads, and I follow; that's the way it's always been. I don't know how to be brave without him."

Orin barked out an incredulous bite of laughter, sweeping his arm in a broad gesture encompassing the entire ship. "You've given everything you have to a no-account bastard pilot and flung yourself headfirst over the Verge to find your brother. You're so brave it's downright foolhardy."

Ari gripped harder at the door panel, flexing his fingers in agitation. "It's no less than he would have done for me."

Orin's dimples popped in his right cheek, twinkle briefly appearing through the murky haze of fear. "Sugar, all that tells me is that you're both extraordinary."

Ari pulled strength from the rush of warmth that ran through him at the words. He released the panel as he stepped back and said with a determined if somewhat shaky breath, "Alright. I'll be ready."

As the door shut between them, Orin's focus never left his face, his hand half extended almost as if he'd intended to reach for Ari one more time.

The locks spun into place, shockingly loud in the booming silence of the cockpit.

Ari sat in the pilot's seat, one hand gripping the throttle and the other his pistol.

The muffled sounds of Orin banging around and cursing came through the steel of the door. Ari closed his eyes for a moment, breathing deeply against the nausea and fear, trying to picture Theo's smile. Orin's face, complete with dimples, popped up alongside, as if making room for himself in Ari's thoughts.

Ari opened his eyes after a few more seconds, and the gun dropped from his numb fingers. It skidded noisily across the floor as ice entered his veins.

Right in front of him, through the view screen, there was a, well, Ari supposed one could call it a ship.

It was an amalgamation of several smaller ships all chopped into jagged pieces and welded together into this monstrosity, huge and hideous and headed straight for them.

As Ari watched in frozen horror, part of the ship broke off, leaving chunks of debris scattered around as it veered away and propelled toward their ship at an alarming speed.

Delilah shuddered all around him as if echoing his fear.

Ari gripped the throttle at the first hint of motion, throwing them forward with a hard push. He choked out a sob of relief as they hurtled from the ship in a burst of speed, Orin's triumphant shout muffled through the door.

They sped away at full throttle until Delilah shuddered once more before falling back into utter stillness, half of the dash blinking off with a high-frequency drone.

The silence after that was even louder than before.

The cockpit rocked with the horrific screeching sound of metal scraping together as the other ship pulled flush.

Ari held his breath, falling to his knees to scramble for his pistol under the dash when he heard the bay doors opening, lasers discharging immediately.

There was so much shouting, then a loud thump, and then two, and then it sounded as if someone were dragging crates across the floor, metal screaming in protest above the men's voices.

Ari could feel the butt of his pistol just peeking out from where it was wedged beneath the dash. He stretched his fingers toward it, sweaty hand slipping on the smooth pearl handle.

It sounded like someone was tearing panels off the wall, shaking the entire ship with the force of their destruction.

The door to the cockpit opened so quietly Ari might not have noticed if he hadn't been staring at it in abject terror.

A pair of large boots filled the doorway, scuffed and scarred and plated with chrome.

"Well, what do we have here? Already on his knees. Convenient."

Ari had the handle pinched between his two middle fingers, but it slipped out of his grasp when he was yanked to his feet by the back of the neck.

The man was barely taller than him, but twice as wide. The blood drained from Ari's face as he caught his pale eyes, caged behind a transparent yellow visor welded into the man's ruddy flesh at his temples. Wires crawled out like spider legs at each joint, some of them extending down to his jaw.

"I think we might have scored a Doll this time," he called to his companion, stepping back out of the cockpit with Ari in tow.

All traces of numbness left Ari at the sight of Orin sprawled and bleeding on the floor.

Ari began to struggle in earnest, kicking wildly and clawing at his captor. To his stomach-churning horror, a chunk of the man's forearm skin came away beneath Ari's fingers, exposing overlapping metal plates smeared with blood and a clear viscous fluid.

"Aw shit, fucking Doll's gonna make me have to get regloved. Here, you take him."

He shoved Ari at the other man, taller but thinner, teeth blindingly white against his pitted dark skin. More than blindingly white. They were actually glowing, phosphorescent.

Ari was distracted enough by the preternaturally glowing teeth that the man was able to bring his wrists together in front of him to slap him in cuffs, extending painfully from his wristbone to halfway up his forearms. He clamped his lips together against the awful sound that wanted to escape, clawing at his throat like a caged wild thing.

Glowing Teeth shoved Ari away, laughing as he stumbled in a desperate attempt to avoid stepping on Orin's hand.

Yellow Visor circled Ari, scanning him critically before turning to prod Orin's still form with his boot. "This one's Verge trash, all marked up. Damaged goods. We'll throw him in with the dents and scratches. The mines will take him for a decent price, at least, with that size."

Relief flooded Ari at the confirmation that Orin was alive. He had been burning holes in his broad back as he watched and waited for it to rise and fall. It did, but slowly and shallowly. He stared down at Orin's soft brown hair, his head turned the other way so Ari couldn't even see his face.

Yellow Visor turned back to Ari, boots screeching against the floor with a metallic crunch at every step. "This one though. He's a perfect little Doll. Core bred and soft as anything."

Ari tried to jerk away as he flicked out a knife, cutting Ari's shirt open across his belly before sliding his hand under the waistband of Ari's trousers to dig dirty fingertips into the vulnerable hollow of Ari's hip.

Acid rose in his throat as he tried to pull away, some of that sound escaping his lips, burning all the way out.

"All this fine virgin skin. Not a mark on him. Some house will be happy to put their brand down; it should stand out really nice on his pasty ass. We'll get a good payout on this one, mark my words."

Glowing Teeth grunted, digging the fingers of one hand into the wires embedded in the opposite elbow with a horribly wet clicking sound. "Better be a good payout. This Verge rat's gonna be hell to lift. Come on, man, let's get them loaded and see if Toya wants to take on their shitty little ship. You can play with the Doll on your own time. They creep me the fuck out."

He bent into a squat and hooked his arms under Orin's shoulders, elbows bending with the sound of a ratchet wrench, before standing with another loud grunt and dragging Orin toward the bay doors like a massive rag doll.

Orin's knees knocked hard against the threshold, and Ari rushed to lift one of his legs with his cuffed hands, trying to keep him from further injury.

Yellow Visor laughed as he pulled Ari away, his damaged arm still leaking rivulets of blood and thick globs of fluid, punishingly tight around Ari's waist.

"You hear that, Doll? You and me are gonna get to play. Guess I should probably warn you, I never learned to play nice."

Chapter Twenty-Two

Orin would bust this ship apart rivet by rivet. He'd rip the bastards' heads off. He'd tear the flesh from his own bones if he needed to. Just see if he wouldn't.

These Outlier scumbags didn't know what a man raised in the Verge colonies was capable of.

Orin had lived through things that would make their metal-riddled skin crawl. Make them weep and beg and cower just like he had. Like the snot-nosed little boy he'd been.

Well, now the boy had grown into a mountain. And the mountain was pissed.

He spat out an acrid mouthful of blood onto the rust-streaked floor, flexing against the restraints, the first band clamped around his biceps to pull his elbows behind his back and the second row tight around his wrists.

Thing was, these raiders were cheap bastards. Used inexpensive standard restraints, mass produced, one-size-fits-most garbage.

Orin wasn't most, turned out. And he'd been in this situation before, just with a lot less to lose. Now he had to bide his time, make sure he could get to Ari before he busted out of these.

He flexed again just to feel them strain, the telltale creak of overstretched joints letting him know just where he was going to need to put the most pressure when the time came.

Pushing to his feet, he took position beside the door at the *thump-clank-scrape* of steps approaching. At least two sets of boots.

He pressed his straining shoulder into the wall beside the door, debating whether it was better to go ahead and bust out of his cuffs or wait and see.

The soft sound of a familiar voice making a stifled noise of protest settled the debate.

Orin wasn't going to make a single move that might endanger Aristotle.

The door slid halfway open, Ari tumbling inside like he'd been pressed against it, barely drawing his legs back in time for it to slide shut again with a reverberating clang.

Ari's harsh breath filled the room as he used his cuffed hands to balance himself on his knees, head swiveling anxiously.

The only light provided was the strobing ceiling panel, casting him in alternating washes of yellow light and deepened shadow.

Orin stepped away from the door, and Ari's breath caught on a sob, hands lifting to reach for him.

Orin nearly fell to his knees, arms throwing him off balance as he rushed over, drinking in Ari's face.

"Did they touch you, honey? Did they put their filthy rusted hands on you?"

Ari ignored the question as his hands ran all over Orin's head, fingers drifting across his face before squeezing at his stiff shoulders, sweet little face creased with concern.

Sweet little face not marked up with anything else, thank the stars.

Orin ducked his head to meet his eyes, voice all busted up gravel in his throat. "Answer me."

Ari shook his head, hands still roaming over Orin's face like he didn't quite know he was doing it. "No. No one has hurt me. They have orders to leave me—I believe the term was—intact."

Orin nodded like he believed him, but he caught a flash of pale skin through a deliberate slit cut into his shirt. Fresh copper flooded his mouth as he bit his cheek at the sight.

First man he found with a knife on him better say his prayers.

Speaking of.

"Listen, sugar. I'm gonna need you to do something for me right quick. Reach behind me and feel at the rear clip of my braces. There's a little catch on the side next to my skin, just big enough to push a fingernail into. Can you press that for me? I can usually get it in wristcuffs, but these armbands are tripping me up a little."

Ari blinked in confusion, hands falling to his lap. "For what purpose?"

Orin rolled his eyes, scuffling around on his knees to present his back to Ari. "Obviously, I'm trying to get those pretty little fingers in my pants. Thought right here and now was a good time to be getting amorous. Nah, I got a little blade in there I need you to get out for me."

Ari's hands slid carefully into the back of his trousers, the rounded bulk of his cuffs pressing uncomfortably into Orin's lower back as he shifted his fingers this way and that, searching for the catch.

His forehead rested between Orin's shoulder blades, voice soft and breath warm through the thin linen of his shirt.

"I do apologize, Orin. I don't seem especially adept at this. I'm afraid I'm finding it terribly difficult to locate. I'm not sure if— Oh!"

His little exclamation was barely a puff of air against Orin's back, drowned out by the click of his brace blade coming loose in his hands.

Ari drew his hand out of Orin's trousers with extreme care, sitting back on his heels to examine the blade. It was thin and narrow, just about the size of Ari's ring finger.

Orin shuffled back around, spinning the odds in his head as he thought through every way he might get them out of there alive and unshackled.

Not but one way he could think of really. Might as well get started now.

Ari held the blade out to him on his palm, as if offering an after-dinner sweet. Orin shook his head.

"Nah, baby, that's for you to get out of those cuffs. Bring your wrists up here so I can get a good look at them."

Ari lifted his arms, wincing as they raised over his shoulder.

Someone was going to lose an augment or two over that wince. Orin was going to send pieces of bloody machinery flying through the dark after this.

He examined Ari's cuffs, asking him to turn this way or that to get a better angle. Took a minute, but Orin finally nodded, relieved these weren't the kind you couldn't get out of without breaking some bones.

"Okay, here's what you're gonna do. You hand me that blade, and I'll hold it steady for you. Then you're gonna bash those cuffs against the floor just as hard as you can right there on that red stripe. Once they get a crack, you're gonna wedge the blade in and pry them open just enough to slip out. Might scrape a bit, but you've got narrow little hands, should come out easy."

Ari nodded, following his instructions to the letter, with a moment of difficulty in getting them to crack. Orin loved watching his little face scrunch with determination as he kept on trying without a whine, solid steel spine under all that delicate beauty.

Once Ari's hands were free, if a little red and scraped raw, he took the blade from Orin's fingers, feeling over Orin's cuffs with his dominant hand.

"Alright, now tell me how to do yours."

Orin shook his head, twisting his body around to Ari. "Not doing mine yet."

Ari crawled over to face him, blade clutched carefully in his hand.

"Whyever not? It seems to me you would be far more of an asset than I am. I assumed I was removing my cuffs in order to better remove yours."

Orin shook his head again. "No, see, they're gonna come back in here pretty soon, and if they see me swinging my arms, they'll just stun us both down. You take that blade, and you're gonna wait by the door. When it opens, I'm gonna rush the bastards, bowl them over on their metal asses. Bust out of my cuffs while I'm busting heads. Meanwhile, you run and take the first ship you find away from here."

Ari's face darkened, and he dropped the blade to the floor with a quiet ping. His hands were steady and purposeful as he felt over Orin's scalp.

"I believe you may have suffered a head injury. Because surely that is the only possible explanation for your presenting me with a plan that involves me leaving you trussed up here to be sold like a pig at the market."

Orin butted his head against Ari's palm, carefully arranging his face into a cocky grin.

"Aw, now, don't you worry about me. I'll knock 'em all flat and make my way home in my own time. You go on and find your brother."

Ari's intelligent eyes burned into Orin's face, melting away the grin like a layer of wax. "You're lying. You don't think you can get out of this, and you're lying to get me to leave you here."

Orin finally lost it. In the back of his mind, he knew he came across like a wild beast, teeth bared and bloody, massive shoulders rounded painfully backward by his arms lashed tightly behind him. He just couldn't care any longer.

He pushed his face up to Ari's, putting every ounce of authority he ever had into his voice. "Do as I say, damn it. We'll only get one chance."

Ari rested his hands on Orin's chest, face drained of all color, freckles like specks of blood spattered in the snow. "I'm not going to run like a coward and abandon you to these barbarians! How could you—?"

"Please. Baby." Orin's voice grated rough and sharp over Ari's objections, stripped down to his bones with nothing left but honesty. "Please. Do this for me. This one last thing."

Ari's face crumpled, tears connecting the dots between his freckles. He petted at Orin's face and hair like he was something precious. His soft touch hurt Orin worse than the ache in his arms. "I don't suppose there's much chance that you have another spouse hidden among the raiders?" His voice cracked and wobbled around the edges of his attempt at lightness.

Orin chuckled weakly, letting his face fall into the cup of Ari's hands. "'Fraid not, sugar."

Ari nodded absently as he catalogued Orin's face with the same level of concentration Orin had seen him devote to his rocks. No detail left unnoticed under all that brilliance.

Ari wiped at the tears on his face and traced the line of Orin's jaw with damp fingers.

"I love you," he said, and it slipped over every inch of Orin just like silk, so smooth and so soft that it flowed right across all his ugly places, whispered over his jagged edges where he always thought it would snag and tear and get ruined.

It didn't. It wasn't ruined. It was right there, in those eyes. Huge and green and fair shining with the words.

"I love you," Ari said again, like maybe Orin didn't hear him right the first time. Like those words in that voice wouldn't be ringing in his ears until his dying day.

Orin collapsed forward, pressing their lips together messy and soft and as sweet as he could make it with the taste of blood still in his mouth, whispering secrets like a cup spilling over with honeyed wine.

"Sweetheart. You don't even know how much I love you. Adore you. Cherish you, baby. So much I can hardly breathe for all the love I got for you, filling up my chest with hearts and flowers and stars-be-damned poetry. Mixing up my mind 'til you're all I can think of. All the time."

Ari laughed, and the sound mended something in Orin's bones, something cracked and aching for so long he barely noticed it anymore.

Orin was so light and lifted he almost didn't hear the sounds of feet approaching.

Chapter Twenty-Three

Ari shifted in place beside the door, trying to keep his broken cuffs balanced around his wrists, small blade clutched in his clammy fist.

Orin stood in front of the doorway, head down and knees bent like a bull about to charge.

Ari's chest clenched painfully as the small grid on the top of the door slid open, revealing just a hint of glow from the raider's bizarre teeth.

"Got a buyer already." Glowing Teeth sounded upbeat, almost chipper. "You're lucky Park's crew was in the market for some muscle as well as a Doll for his house. Sounds like you'll be kept together a little while longer, lovebirds."

He opened the door noisily, a small bolt shimmying free from the scarred surface and bouncing on the floor with a metallic ping. The odd conical barrel of his pistol entered the room before he did, wavering for a moment before settling on pointing at Ari, the raider's smug grin glowing Orin's way.

Orin's jaw clenched, acid glare burning into the raider's skull.

Glowing Teeth stepped inside the room to reveal another man waiting silently in the doorway.

The man looked dangerous, dark eyes hard and flat in his rawboned face, black ink climbing over his skin out of every edge of his clothing like smoke escaping. Up his neck and down over his hands, strange patterns of intersecting parallel lines with small circles and hexagons and— And Hangul. There. Across his knuckles where he held a charged laser pistol at the ready.

Ari sucked in a breath so sharp he choked, coughing violently, grip tightening around the little blade in his hands as he stared up at his brother's abductor.

It made a horrific sort of sense now. Hearing all of this talk of Ari's value as a Core-born Doll, whatever that meant. Theo must be equally valued, and it appeared this Park was a slave trader, the lowest form of scum in the dark.

Ari could only hope Theo was still aboard his ship when Ari and Orin were brought on.

Orin planted his feet, muscles tight with determination. Ari shook his head frantically, wishing he could tell Orin what he had discovered. Orin's face creased in confusion, but his stance relaxed somewhat, assuring Ari he was no longer preparing to charge.

Ari needed this man to lead him to Theo. This was his best chance, falling into his lap like serendipity holding a laser pistol to his head.

Park was arguing with Glowing Teeth now, deep voice spitting angry words in some language Ari had never heard before. Glowing Teeth shoved against his chest, but the man didn't move an inch.

Park stepped back before calmly administering a swift kick to Glowing Teeth's chest, sending the man scraping across the floor with a shout, wires ripping out of his arms and legs in a shower of sparks and fluids.

Park spat out another string of words in that language before Glowing Teeth held up a hand, scowling at his loose wires peevishly.

"Alright, alright. Like I give a shit as long as I get paid. You gotta load them up though, I'm not touching that huge Verge fucker again; he weighs a metric assload."

Park turned directly to Ari then, something unreadable flickering in his hooded eyes. "Come with me. Both of you. Now."

Ari followed him out, Orin right at his heels, already glaring daggers at Park's back. If only they had a moment to themselves so Ari could explain what he had just discovered about their new captor.

Nausea rolled in his stomach, a terrible chemical reaction of excitement at the possibility of being reunited with Theo and absolute dread at the possibility he could already be gone. Sold off wherever this evil man did such despicable business.

They followed him out onto a small ship, only slightly bigger than Delilah but significantly older, exterior dented and scraped down into a rough patchwork made up of countless layers of paint and rust.

Park gestured to an emergency seat bolted into the dingy wall. "You, redhead, sit down and buckle up." His gaze slid to Orin disdainfully. "Verge trash can sit on the floor."

The doors shut behind him with a loud shriek of scraping metal as he left them there, engines thrumming underfoot.

Ari sat on the chair, buckling in as Orin sank onto the floor at his feet, shoulder pressed to the outside of Ari's thigh.

Ari pulled a hand out of his cuffs, reached down to run his fingers through Orin's hair, then held his head still as he leaned in as though to give him a kiss. Instead, he whispered urgently against Orin's mouth, "This is the man I've been searching for, this Park. This is the man who took Theo; I'm certain of it."

Orin sucked in a harsh breath, the rough scrape of scabbed-over lips pressing to Ari's as he said in a quiet rumble, "So we're just biding our time to see if he leads us to your brother?"

"Precisely." Ari sat back up but left his hand to card through Orin's hair. He braced him against his leg as the ship took off with a terrifying wobble and headed jerkily away from the raider ship.

Orin barked out a harsh laugh, scorn dripping from every word. "This asshole can't even fly. We're pulling to the aft from some piece of junk he's hauling, and he's not even correcting for it. Idiot probably couldn't fly a paper plane on a rusted stick."

Ari gave a tiny smile at Orin's outrage, petting his poor, stiff shoulders as his mind reeled with the possibilities. Scenarios ran through his head one after another, ranging from the terrible to the sublime, layering over one another into a tangled mess.

There was a very good chance Theo wasn't even being held by this man any longer. That he had been sent away somewhere Ari might not be able to follow. The thought tasted like ashes.

And here Ari was, leading Orin further into trouble for his own selfish reasons. Without Ari, Orin could probably escape, get back to his life as it was before Ari came crashing in with his half-baked plans and naive suppositions.

If Ari were a better man, he would tell him to go, leave Ari behind.

But without the ship, Ari had nothing of significant value with which to pay him what he was owed. Ari was not in the habit of accumulating debt. Orin deserved so much better.

If only Theo were here. Decisive, impulsive Theo. Theo didn't believe in hesitation or regret. Theo would rather set a course blindly and charge forward than ever sit and agonize over his options, like Ari was now.

Useless, timid Ari. What was he going to do if he didn't find Theo wherever this Park scoundrel was taking them? How was he ever going to find him if this last, all-important lead brought them to a dead end?

Orin shifted beside him, scanning the room slowly and methodically, like he was making a map in his head. He had spent hours now, bound in those uncomfortable cuffs, not a complaint to be heard. He deserved better than the faltering mess Ari was rapidly spiraling into.

Ari closed his eyes, pulled something out from the ever-deepening well within himself, something resolute, adding starch to his spine until he sat up as straight as perfect collar points.

He would be strong, for Orin, and brave, for Theo. For as long as it was required of him. He could do no less. It was the very least they deserved.

They deserved far more than he could give, the both of them, but unfortunately all they had was Ari, so he resolved to make the best of himself.

There were minerals, after all, which had the ability to change under pressure. Develop new traits—greater strength, hardness, durability. Ari would take his inspiration from them.

He would not crumble under pressure.

Their docking was not quite as smooth as their takeoff. Which was to say, it was absolutely abysmal. The ship shook and wobbled, veering wildly off to one side as they docked, the shrill scrape of metal on metal all around them.

Orin offered a running commentary of events in a biting tone Ari had never heard him use before.

"Coming in too fast, idiot's gonna. Yep. Busted up his own loading dock. Oughta paint a target on it, if this is how he's gonna fly. I bet this fool couldn't hit the floor falling out of bed. Now he's overcorrected, and we're gonna. Yep. Bottom out and dust the floor with metal shavings. No wonder his rusted ship looks like somebody took a bite out of it. Miracle we made it in one piece, with him flying."

Ari stifled a giggle at Orin's indignation, and Orin glanced up with a tilt of his lips that let Ari know he was doing it on purpose. Exaggerating his outrage to get Ari's mind off their troubles for a brief moment.

Ari hadn't known it was possible to love somebody so much, so quickly. And yet the evidence was incontrovertible, thumping right there in Ari's chest.

Somehow, miraculously, answered in those honey eyes.

The door to the cockpit opened with a reluctant squeal, stifling every last drop of laughter left in Ari's throat as he quickly tucked his wrists back into his cuffs, shifting them to appear as intact as possible.

Park stepped out of the cockpit, sharp gaze falling immediately to Ari's broken cuffs. Orin stiffened at his side, then pushed to his feet, his own cuffs groaning in protest.

Ari held his breath, clutching his little blade.

Park stared Ari down, one dark eyebrow lifting incrementally. "You can take those off now." His gaze slid to Orin, face hardening. "Both of you. If you can keep your guard dog to heel."

Metal squealed and groaned as Orin threw himself back against the wall with a loud *thunk,* arm cuffs cracking open at the sides.

Ari stood, and his own cuffs crashed to the floor as he hurried to help. "Wait, wait. You'll hurt yourself. Allow me to assist."

Orin's wristcuffs were already cracked open, but Ari was able to pry them open further until Orin could slip out without losing much skin. Orin took the blade from Ari and shoved him behind his back as he stood to face Park, huge fists raised menacingly.

Park watched them dispassionately, free hand reaching out to open the bay doors without looking at the panel, unimpressed eyes trained on Orin's fists.

The bay doors opened with a rusty screech and the ramp clattered down into a large cargo bay crammed full of mismatched crates.

Park gestured to the ramp with his pistol, something like anticipation moving across his face and churning Ari's guts.

Orin moved to walk down, but Park called out to stop him.

"No. Redhead goes first."

Orin snarled at Park over his shoulder, but Ari slipped his hand into Orin's and started down the ramp with a suppressed shudder at Park's expectant expression.

Noises in the cluttered cargo bay indicated the presence of more people, although some of the uncoordinated clamoring sounded more like a herd of puppies strapped into combat boots and running down the stairs.

The invisible puppies skidded across the floor behind the stacks, bumping into crates and knocking something small over with a muffled crash.

Park lifted the hand that wasn't holding the pistol to pinch at the low bridge of his nose, eyes squeezing shut at the sound.

Someone rounded the corner of a stack of crates at breakneck speed, thin form clothed from head to toe in skintight black clothing in the same bizarre make as Park's, with a soft gray hood pulled low over their head.

They stopped a few feet away, pale hand reaching up to clutch at their chest as they threw back their hood.

Ari let go of Orin's hand, his entire body engulfed in alternating waves of heat and ice, limbs shaking and knees turned to water.

He stumbled like a baby deer as he ran into his brother's arms.

Chapter Twenty-Four

Ari pulled away to stare into a set of achingly familiar green eyes, his view slightly obscured by the messy strands of long red hair that fell in front of them.

The room wavered as tears filled Ari's vision, spilling hot against his cheeks. His lips moved ineffectually, unable to form words properly with all of the air punched out of his lungs.

Of course, when Theo was around, no one else generally needed words as he was always more than willing to fill every silence.

"Ari! Don't cry, darling! Oh, but I have missed you terribly, every moment of every day! You wouldn't believe the adventure I have been having. It has been ever so exciting. And now that you are here, it shall be even better. Stand back and let me look at you."

Ari took a dutiful if somewhat wobbly step backward, hands and feet still numb with shock, and Orin pressed up close behind him as though offering him something solid to lean upon. Ari sagged against him gratefully as Theo took his hands and held them out between them, checking him over carefully, forehead scrunching with concern.

"A trifle the worse for wear, aren't you? No matter; I'll have you spit spot and back to your old self in no time at all. All you need is a touch of pomade and a deft hand with the needle to repair those clothes." Theo pursed his lips, scanning Ari up and down. "Or perhaps an incinerator and a trip to my own wardrobe would be more in order. But, do tell, who is your handsome stranger? You haven't landed yourself into trouble, have you, Ari? I must say, that isn't very like you." Theo blotted Ari's cheeks with the soft material of his sleeve.

Ari gestured behind him, accidentally connecting with Orin's chest with an audible slap, his mind a chaotic swirl of joy and confusion, voice catching in his throat.

"Oh, I—I do apologize. Allow me to introduce Mr. Orin Stone, my most capable pilot. Mr. Stone, my brother, Dr. Theophrastus Campbell."

Orin retreated a step at Ari's words, as if belatedly remembering to put space between them. Ari glanced over his shoulder at him in bewilderment, but his attention was returned to Theo as he made a thoughtful, and, for him, ominous hum.

Theo's thoughtful hums only ever led directly to disaster.

To Ari's astonishment, Theo seemed quite his usual self, entirely unchanged by his ordeal, if one were to discount his strange apparel. One would never have known he had recently been the unwilling victim of a terrible crime against his person.

Then again, Theo had always been rather resilient in nature.

Orin still stood close enough behind him that Ari could feel the rumble of his voice run up his spine like a bolstering hand. "Pleased to meet you, Theo. Nice to be able to put a face to the name."

Theo sparkled up at Orin with a cheeky grin. "Charmed, Mr. Stone."

Laughter colored Theo's voice in a warm tone Ari had been terrified of never hearing again, the sound of it filling his hidden wells of sadness as if they had never been.

Theo turned back to Ari with a waggle of his eyebrows that was the polar opposite of subtle, one slim finger tapping at the tip of Ari's nose lightly. "I have found that one can benefit from a spot of trouble now and again, wouldn't you agree?"

Ari's mind finally snapped into focus as Park stepped closer, the lurking bulk of his black-clad form reminding Ari of the danger they were in with a sudden chill through his bones.

He pushed Theo behind him with shaking hands, Orin tensing and moving by his side immediately, small blade held out between his massive knuckles. "Don't worry, Theo, we will liberate you from this villain!" Ari assured him in a voice that hardly shook at all.

Theo just walked around him, cocking his head to check Ari over in uncharacteristic silence before turning to point a finger at Park, advancing on him at a rate Ari found inadvisable, long locks of hair whipping behind his head like the vengeful snakes of a gorgon.

"You didn't tell them you were rescuing them?" Theo yelled, digging his finger into the solid wall of Park's chest, appearing entirely unfazed by Park's fearsome scowl.

Park shrugged, face a portrait of unconcern as he scratched at his chin with the barrel of his pistol. "No."

Theo waved his arms like he might yet discover the secret of flight, smacking the back of one against the meat of Park's shoulder but receiving no visible reaction from Park in return.

"Whyever not?" Theo's voice squeaked beneath the sheer force of his indignation, hands continuing to churn up the air around him.

Park shrugged again, tucking his pistol into the holster under his arm as he leveled dark eyes on Theo, just a hint of a smile crinkling them at the corners.

"It was funny."

Theo frowned, settling his weight back on one heel as he crossed his arms over his chest, glaring at Park.

"You can't do that to him! Ari isn't like me. He's sensitive. Sweet. Dare I say, unassuming. Easily frightened. Picture a helpless baby rabbit with a rock collection, and you would have my brother. You cannot treat him like this and expect to get away with it; I won't let you. He doesn't have the constitution to put up with your nonsense, Jun!"

Ari stared at Theo, a wave of every terrible feeling he had endured since his brother's disappearance rising up inside of him, bringing him to an absolute boil.

"I'm sorry. Was dropping everything and jumping the Verge in desperate search of you not brave enough, Theo?" Words tumbled out of his mouth like hot lava before he could stop himself. "Should I have perhaps done the whole thing blindfolded with my hands tied behind my back? Although, I did spend a shocking amount of time in wristcuffs, now that I think on it." Ari's voice petered out at the same rate as his anger, ending on a quiet mumble directed at Theo's steel-capped toes.

Theo remained unaffected by Ari's outburst, mouth quirking up slyly, gaze sliding from Ari to Orin and back. "Oh, did you? How interesting," he said, voice like treacherous silk.

Ari blanched, glancing over at Orin to find his face nearly split in half by amusement, every dimple on full display as he watched their exchange, thumbs looped in his braces and giving every appearance of enjoying himself thoroughly.

The little blade was nowhere to be seen, presumably tucked back into its hiding place.

Ari's face burned as Theo and Orin's grins just grew wider and wider.

"No. Not like— Nothing like that. We were held by Enforcers and raiders, and then your Mr. Park here. It was all very harrowing, I assure you."

Park's face twisted into a forbidding frown at that. "Captain Park." His deep voice cut, sharp vowels hinting at the accent Theo had written into his notes. "And I'm not his."

Theo's grin fell away as he squinted up at Captain Park, who appeared to be making a concerted effort not to look back at him, instead turning away to walk behind the dented ship he had brought them in.

Theo followed for a few steps before throwing his hands up in the air, voice tight with exasperation. "Where exactly do you think you are going? We have guests to accommodate!"

Captain Park threw his words over his shoulder like a dagger. "I'm unhooking your stupid little ship."

Orin perked up at the words, casting Ari an excited glance before trotting over behind the ship after Captain Park.

His joyful exclamation sent answering joy sparking through Ari, followed by distress, and immediately after, shame.

Orin started crooning love songs to Delilah as Ari's heart sank deeper and deeper into the toes of his boots. If Captain Park had brought their ship along, then that meant— Well. It meant everything was as it should be, to Ari's disgraceful despair.

He followed them, rounding Park's beat-up rescue vessel just as Theo caught up to him, linked their arms, and rested his head on Ari's shoulder. Ari could feel how much he had missed him in the tense grip of his fingers around Ari's arm, like he was afraid of letting go even for a second.

Theo was ever the one to run his mouth, but when it came to his true feelings, they were best expressed through his actions. Words were the armor he hid behind, just as solitude had always been for Ari.

Would soon be again, it would seem.

Ari covered Theo's hand on his arm, squeezing lightly. "How are you, truly, Theo?" He pitched his words to be kept just between them. "You must tell me if you have come to any harm."

Theo shook his head, rolling his bony skull against Ari's shoulder and tickling his neck with his unruly hair.

"No harm at all. Nothing worth noting anyway. The Captain has done his best to keep me safe, and he can be quite formidable when he puts his mind to it. You should see him in action, Ari, he's like a dancer. That is, if the dancer were bristling with weapons and maintained a perpetual black mood. And absolutely despised dancing. And music, for that matter. He's actually not much like a dancer, upon further consideration."

Something clanged to the floor beneath Delilah, swiftly followed by a shout from Orin and a scathing reply from Park.

Ari continued, keeping his voice low, "This Captain Park, Theo. Was I wrong in surmising that you were taken by him unwillingly? I have been chasing after him for weeks now, only to find that you appear to be something like his friend."

Theo shook his head again, lifting it from Ari's shoulder with a tight smile that reached for his eyes but never quite connected. His fingers remained clutched tight to Ari's arm.

"I will tell him you said that; he will not be pleased to hear he gave you such an impression. His face will be an absolute delight. As for my abduction. I suppose one could say, technically, you were correct. I wouldn't say I was abducted entirely unwillingly, however. It was quite late in the evening, and I was exceedingly bored. You know how I get when I am in need of diversion, Ari."

Ari took a step back to gape at him through a fog of ever-growing consternation, pain radiating between his temples in the beginnings of a very familiar Theo-shaped headache.

Theo continued on, oblivious, "Alright. So yes, he did abduct me. But as it turns out, he had a very good reason for doing so. Well, perhaps not for kidnapping me at gunpoint. That was a bit of a faux pas on his part. We have since grown past it, as you can see. He could have simply asked for my assistance, which I have made clear to him would have been the better choice. He isn't terribly good with words, I'm afraid, but he does have other redeeming qualities, I assure you."

Ari took a deep breath, counted to three, then exhaled noisily, prying Theo's fingers from his arm to hold them tightly in his hand.

"Theo. By all that is holy, tell me you have not fallen in love with him."

Theo winced, lips twisted into a hopeful curve that boded ill for the structural integrity of Ari's stomach lining. "No?" he tried, sounding entirely unsure. "No. Absolutely not. Of course not, Ari, don't be a goose." His certainty appeared tissue-thin.

Ari had hoped for a more unequivocal answer because when Theo fell in love, it was a bit like a natural disaster. Swift, brutal, and leaving a trail of destruction in its path that Ari usually had to be the one to tidy up.

Theo beamed at him, squeezing his hand between both of his, a slight chill from the loading bay clinging to his thin fingers. "And besides, Ari, just see how wonderful it has been for you to go on this adventure! Now that I have you before me, I can tell I did the right thing in leaving those clues. I did worry it might be too much for you, but here you are, altogether radiant from the experience! I would say it was rather good for you to get out of the house, regardless of the less than ideal circumstances."

Ari had once read the phrase "seeing red" in an overblown gothic novel and had scoffed at the description. How ridiculous, the notion that rage could alter one's visual perception.

Now, as Theo happily declared himself to have been quite clever for setting them both upon such a wonderful adventure, Ari saw red.

He dropped Theo's hand, stumbling back a pace, and then another, until his heel scattered something small and metallic across the metal grating of the floor.

"You thought—you thought it would be good for me. To get out of the house. You dare say those words to me in that order? Now? After all I have done for you?"

Theo's smile fell in little increments as if someone were dialing back the brightness on their screen, hands slowly raising between them in a gesture of consolation that was far too little, far too late.

Ari jutted his chin, hands rolling into fists as he held his arms stiff at his sides, attempting to control his breathing before he screamed.

Theo's face paled as Ari set his jaw, hands now held out between them as if asking Ari to take them into his own. "Oh, don't give me the chin, Ari! You cannot tell me it hasn't been a grand adventure. I would indeed say it has been good for you. Just consider how far you have gotten out of your comfort zone! And with a strapping young man at your side, no less." Theo threw him a wink that might as well have been a lit match on a barrel of fuel crystals.

Ari silently counted to three, and then five, and then ten. Then he took a deep breath and launched himself at his brother, hands and hair flying.

Theo shrieked, covering his face as the pair fell to the ground, Ari immediately sitting up on Theo's stomach to slap at every inch of him he could reach, shouting at him between every slap.

"You! Absolute! Idiot! How *could* you!? You. Could. Have. Died! I'm going to *kill* you!"

Theo reached up and snagged Ari's hair, prompting Ari to grab a fistful of Theo's longer hair and yank until they both had tears in their eyes, snarling in each other's faces.

Ari had to let go with an indignant squawk as he was lifted off his twin by one thick arm and held immobile against Orin's chest as he fought to catch his breath. He glared at Theo where he sat on the ground, rubbing his head angrily and glaring back at Ari.

Ari felt more than saw Orin jerk his head at Park.

"Go on, Captain, see to yours. Seems like whatever this hullabaloo is about, we won't be settling it like adults."

Ari slowly turned his head on his neck like an owl to stare incredulously up at the pilot who had, not a half hour before, been ready to brawl at a moment's notice with nothing more than a miniscule blade at his disposal.

Theo sniffled piteously as Park helped him to stand with a swift yank on his arm before stepping away and craning his neck to the ceiling with the closest thing to a smile Ari had yet seen flitting across his face.

Theo sniffled again twice as loud, glaring at Park from under damp lashes, face flushed the same burning red as Ari's own skin. "Whatever are you doing?"

Park turned an actual, genuine, extremely brief smile on Theo, gesturing carelessly at the ceiling. "Checking to make sure the cameras got that. They did. I'm thinking of selling copies to the crew."

Theo turned his back on Park rather pointedly, aiming sad puppy eyes in Ari's direction as he rubbed gingerly at his scalp with an exaggerated whimper.

Ari pointed a scornful finger at Theo, boots scrabbling over Orin's shins as he tried to launch himself once more, shoving at the arm holding him still.

"Oh, shut up, Theophrastus. You deserved all that and worse!"

To his annoyance, he could feel Orin battling laughter behind him, the muscles of his abdomen shaking with the effort.

Theo had the nerve to pout, lower lip jutting out and arms crossed tetchily.

Ari mimicked the way Theo liked to toss his hair over his shoulder with a flick of his head, but since Ari had much shorter hair, he only managed to appear as though he were avoiding a fly.

"Look at me!" He pitched his voice in Theo's characteristic upbeat inflection. "I'm Theo, and I think everything is simply marvelous all the time and I never stop to think before making incredibly stupid decisions! I never take the time to consider the consequences of my actions! Aren't I just so fun and whimsical? Isn't everything such a lark?"

Ari dropped his voice to his normal tone, bypassing it completely and continuing on down to a scathing snarl. "You almost got me sold by raiders, Theo! You almost got my—my— My pilot killed!"

Theo's eyes welled with tears, his nose going that unattractive rosy hue that let Ari know they were genuine, and Ari's rage deflated like it had been stuck by a pin. "I'm sorry, Aristotle. Truly. I should never have made light of things. I really have missed you most terribly. Thank you for coming to find me. You are the best brother one could ever wish for."

Orin let him slide to the ground and took his face in one large hand to swipe at his cheeks with a faded plaid handkerchief Ari had never seen before. "I gotta say, this isn't exactly the kind of tearful reunion I was expecting."

Ari hadn't even realized tears were running down his face until Orin was wiping them gently away. He caught Orin's hand in his and held it to his cheek, determinedly ignoring the delighted squeal Theo made behind him. "I can't believe you have your ship. Will she be able to fly again soon, do you think?"

Orin beamed, smile warm against Ari's face like sunshine on a winter's day. He resolved to soak it up as long as he could, storing it away for the cold nights ahead.

"Give me a couple hours with my toolkit, and she'll be right as rain."

Orin's smile faltered as fresh tears overflowed Ari's eyes, dampening their clasped hands.

Ari nodded, trying to keep his expression bright. "Good. That's good. How wonderful for you. You have more than earned it. I suppose the time has come for us to part ways, then. I shall— I'm afraid I shall miss you terribly." Ari choked back a sob, and Orin's fingers tightened across his jaw as he studied Ari solemnly. "I cannot begin to pretend otherwise. You already know that I— You know how I feel. About you. I shall always—always be grateful for our time together."

Orin's face sparkled with a joy Ari found entirely unsuitable for the circumstances. "Sweetheart, for a brilliant scientist, you sure can be thick as molasses when you put your mind to it."

Ari reared back, but Orin's hands followed to wrap around his waist and the nape of his neck. "I beg your pardon?"

Orin drew him in close, fitting Ari against himself like he had been crafted entirely for that purpose.

"I ain't going nowhere. Couldn't get rid of me if you tried, honey. You and me, we're in this together. To the end of the line."

Ari trembled in his arms, waves of relief and bursts of joy filling him to the brim until he thought he might fly apart if not for the anchoring sensation of Orin all around him.

Theo waited until Orin's lips were a hairsbreadth away from Ari's before interrupting cheerfully.

"That's certainly good to hear, because we need your help."

Glossary

Augments–physical augmentations popular in the RS (Restricted Sector) including but not confined to: bionic appendages, sensory enhancements, functional tattoos that connect to the stream.

Britannia–Core planet loosely based on Victorian England, Ari and Theo's home world.

Chip–physical currency used both within and beyond the Verge.

Core–the inner circle of planets protected by the Verge. Includes Britannia, Ari and Theo's home world.

Deep Dark–slang for ungoverned open space outside of the barrier of the Verge.

Disconnects–those living in the RS without augments, a small minority.

Dolls–slaves, usually of a sexual nature, originating from Core planets and traded like collectibles within the RS.

Enforcers–Core military and law enforcement.

Ident–short for identity. An electronic payment system based on body codes such as fingerprint or retinal scan, commonly used in the Core.

Mist—recreational drug in the RS.

Outlier—anyone born outside of the Verge, residing in the Restricted Sector.

Raiders—lawless space pirates, usually found in the deep dark, sometimes part of larger Crews, or crime syndicates back in the RS. Often involved in supplying the mines with indentured servants, or running the Doll or Mist trade.

Regeneration fluid—aka regen. Accelerates healing, commonly used in the Core and RS, scarce resource along the Verge colonies and the deep dark.

Restricted Sector—aka the RS. Populated planets and colonies located beyond the barrier of the Verge. They have been cut off from the Core for centuries.

Singer—informant, Verge colonial slang.

Sonic—alternative method of cleaning without using water.

Stream—RS version of the internet, not available within the Verge.

Verge—a physical energy barrier enclosing the Core planets and surrounding colonies. Also refers to the colonies themselves which line the inner curve of the barrier. The closer to the barrier, the fewer the resources and the lower the social standing.

Verge colonies—settlements along the asteroid belt lining the interior wall of the Verge, circling the inner Core. Limited resources, similar to frontier life.

Verge rat–pejorative term for Verge colonists born outside of the Core.

About the Author

A.C. Thomas left the glamorous world of teaching preschool for the even more glamorous world of staying home with her toddler. Between the diaper changes and tea parties, she escapes into fantastical worlds, reading every romance available and even writing a few herself.

She devours books of every flavor—science fiction, historical, fantasy—but always with a touch of romance because she believes there is nothing more fantastical than the transformative power of love.

Email: acthomasbooks@gmail.com

Facebook: www.facebook.com/acthomaswrites

Twitter: @acthomas_books

Website: www.acthomasbooks.com

Coming Soon from A.C. Thomas

Captivated

The Verge, Book Two (Coming Spring, 2021)

Ding. Ding. Donk.

Theo held his index finger up at the uneven chime of the ancient bell over the door, signaling yet another harried university student bustling into his office after hours. It was practically midnight, hardly the time to ask for an extension.

Honestly, students were the worst part of teaching. Theo didn't know why he'd taken the TA position in the first place.

Okay, yes, he did. But, to be fair, Professor Gladwell looked amazing in his spectacles and fitted waistcoats, and who could blame Theo for going a little glassy-eyed whenever they had private meetings?

Well, Professor Gladwell's wife, for one, probably.

Theo finished his note and dropped his pen into the onyx holder on his desk, preparing to give the student his full attention.

Some of his attention.

Whatever was left over while Theo drifted off on thoughts of the strain Professor Gladwell's buttons were under on a daily basis as they tried to contain all that athleticism. Those poor, poor buttons.

He lifted his head with the bored expectation of finding another skinny, pasty academic struggling to hold armfuls of paper with desperation written all over their ink-smudged face.

In other words, someone like Theo.

This person held a sheaf of papers, and there the resemblance ended to every expectation Theo had.

Perhaps it was time to expand his expectations.

"I'm looking for Dr. Campbell," The stranger's voice curled around Theo's ears like smoke.

Theo smiled up at him, admiring the way the lamplight glinted off of his black hair and deep bronze skin. Stars, but he was a handsome specimen.

With a flip of his hair back over his shoulder, Theo marked his place in his notebook by closing a finger in the pages. "Well you're certainly in the right place for it! Though I suppose that depends on which Dr. Campbell you are looking for. There are three of us in my immediate family alone. Although, Campbell isn't a terribly uncommon name, so there could easily be many more Dr. Campbells that I'm entirely unaware of."

The stranger looked as if he very much regretted initiating this conversation. Theo was, unfortunately, familiar with the expression being directed his way.

The stranger shook his head slightly, as though Theo's chatter were water in his ears. Something else Theo was extremely familiar with.

He loomed closer, casting a wide shadow across Theo's cluttered desk when his bulk blocked out the light beside the door. "Dr. Campbell. Where is he?"

Theo traced the impressive line of the stranger's shoulders underneath his unusual many-layered black leather coat before offering his free hand to shake. "I am

Dr. Campbell, pleased to meet you! My brother is also Dr. Campbell, and my father is Dr. Campbell as well, though they would be less pleased to meet you. Nothing against you, personally, they just aren't terribly fond of interacting with strangers. Or people in general, to be honest. Sometimes I think they can barely tolerate me!"

The stranger winced as if he could relate to the sentiment before quietly responding, "Dr. Campbell has been described as a thin male with green eyes, red hair, and pale skin."

His deep voice sank into Theo's bones like the pleasant rumble of a hovercoach over cobblestones.

Dark, hooded eyes skipped over Theo as his visitor described each feature as though checking off a list in his head, all the while ignoring Theo's offered hand.

Theo dropped it to the desk with a shrug; the slight couldn't hamper his enjoyment of this diversion from his research. "I'm afraid that doesn't narrow it down even the slightest bit. My brother and I are identical twins, and we definitely favor our father, to the eternal dismay of our poor mother. My dismay as well, to be honest. It would have been ever so nice to have her chestnut hair rather than this glaring beacon I've got atop my head. I tend to stick out like a redheaded thumb."

The stranger sucked in a breath through clenched teeth, square jaw held tight as his broad shoulders rose and fell in a long, measured sigh.

Theo felt like sighing himself at the sight. The man really was uncommonly beautiful.

He could happily watch those shoulders move for hours. He even had some suggestions regarding the nature of the movement.

His attention was brought to the desk when the stranger slapped a battered manuscript on top of his notebook—an older heatbound copy, of all things. The stranger's fingers were marked with ink, tattooed on the metacarpals between each knuckle with Hangul letters in beautiful calligraphy. Theo had never seen the like.

The stranger put pressure on the hand he held splayed across the document, pinching the finger Theo had left inside his notebook. He yanked it out hastily as the stranger growled at him. "*This* Dr. Campbell."

Absently shaking his pinched finger, Theo scanned the manuscript. The simulated parchment was stained and rumpled. It appeared to have been dog-eared at the corners over and over again, and the pages bristled with assorted tabs. All signs of a book well loved.

He tried to read the cover page, lifting the stranger's long fingers distractedly with his thumb and forefinger until he was hit by a jolt of recognition, filled to the brim with unexpected delight. "Wherever did you get this? I wrote this years ago during my graduate studies! I'm honestly surprised that anyone outside my thesis committee has even read it. It's such an obscure topic, after all. I had the most terrible time just—"

The stranger's palm slammed back down on top of the document, missing Theo's hand by a hair. "You are this Dr. Campbell?"

It appeared as though he already knew the answer and was dreading it as he squinted dubiously in Theo's direction. There was a slight tremble in the man's fingers as they pressed hard against the sheaf of papers.

The stranger's eyes remained shadowed by his strong brow, but his gaze washed over Theo—a wave of heat, laser-focused and far more intense than the conversation warranted.

A frisson of caution tried to nip at Theo's mind, sounding an awful lot like his brother hissing in his ear about good sense. He shook it off the way he usually did and leaned his chin on his hand to peer up at the stranger through his lashes. "Why, yes, I am. To whom do I have the pleasure of speaking?"

The stranger lifted the manuscript, his fingers unmistakably trembling now as he flipped through pages with a dry rustle of sim-parchment. He held the document open to a passage of translation Theo had featured in his study of long-dead languages and shook it rather rudely in his face. "This. You can read this?"

Theo launched into a recitation of the passage, finishing with a flourishing roll of the tongue. It was rare to find a fellow enthusiast on the topic, particularly one so pleasing to the eye. The stranger seemed unusually passionate about the subject, his breath quickening audibly as Theo rattled off the words of a people long gone.

Theo cocked his head to the side and reached for his pen as he opened his notebook. "If you have an interest in the topic, I keep one of my sources here in my office. Just there, on that shelf." He gestured off to the side where his cluttered bookcase leaned heavily against the wall for much-needed support. "It's titled 'An Annotated Glossary of Dead Languages' by Dr. Fernsby."

The stranger folded his sheaf of papers into his coat and walked to the bookcase in two decisive strides. Theo took the opportunity to study him further, pen hovering above his open notebook.

Quickly flipping past a few dozen sketches of Professor Gladwell standing at his lectern, he found an empty page.

As the stranger turned to face the bookcase, Theo caught a glimpse of black ink trailing up his neck to frame his sharp jawline in an odd geometric pattern of thin parallel lines intersected with tiny circles. He attempted to sketch the tattoos onto his paper.

Even more ink snaked out of the cuffs of his coat, wrapping around his wrists and stamping all the way down to his fingers with that lovely calligraphy scribed across his knuckles. Theo wrote down the characters and translated them to Core Standard in the margins.

Honor on one hand and Valor on the other. Fascinating.

Closer examination revealed a design of clustered hexagonal shapes running up the wrist of his left hand. Theo had just begun to sketch them when the stranger turned back toward him, book clutched in his fist.

Theo had never seen anyone remotely resembling the man; nothing about him said "Core," from his sprawling ink to the look in his eye. He gave the impression of someone midway over a rickety rope bridge, unsure of every step but determined to get across.

Theo couldn't help but find his appearance a little bit dangerous as he took in his severely handsome face framed by unevenly-shaved black hair, all of it underscored by the dramatic sweep of his coat.

The impression was cemented when the man tucked the book away inside his coat and pulled his hand back out with a ray gun pointed in Theo's direction.

Theo's pen dropped a blot of ink onto his notebook as the man stepped closer.

The stranger's eyes were so dark his pupils disappeared into the black of his iris. His unrelenting stare sent shivers down Theo's spine that could not be attributed entirely to fear. "Come with me. Now."